THE ALCHEMIST WAR

BY JOHN SEVEN

STONE ARCH BOOKS
a capstone imprint

The Time-Tripping Faradays
are published by Stone Arch Books
A Capstone Imprint
1710 Roe Crest Drive
North Mankato, Minnesota 56003
www.capstonepub.com

Library of Congress Cataloging-in-Publication Data
Seven, John.
  The alchemist war / by John Seven; illustrated by Craig Phillips.
    p. cm. -- (The time-tripping Faradays)
  Summary: Living in the twenty-fifth century, young Dawkins and
Hypatia Faraday take time travel and technology like the NeuroNet for
granted but in Prague in 1648, they are startled to find a rogue alchemist
who is using advanced technology to change mercury into gold.
  ISBN 978-1-4342-6028-4 (library binding) -- ISBN 978-1-4342-6438-1
(pbk.) -- ISBN 978-1-62370-011-9 (paper over board)
1. Time travel--Juvenile fiction. 2. Alchemy--Juvenile fiction. 3.
Adventure stories. 4. Prague (Czech Republic)--History--17th century--
Juvenile fiction. [1. Time travel--Fiction. 2. Alchemy--Fiction. 3. Adventure
and adventurers--Fiction. 4. Science fiction. 5. Prague (Czech Republic)--
History--17th century--Fiction. 6. Czech Republic--History--17th century--
Fiction.] I. Phillips, Craig, 1975- ill. II. Title.
  PZ7.S5145Alc 2013
  813.6--dc23
                        2012051714

Cover illustration: Craig Philips

Designer: Kay Fraser

Photo-Vector Credits: Shutterstock

Printed in the United States of America in Stevens Point, Wisconsin.
032014   008060R

FOR JANA

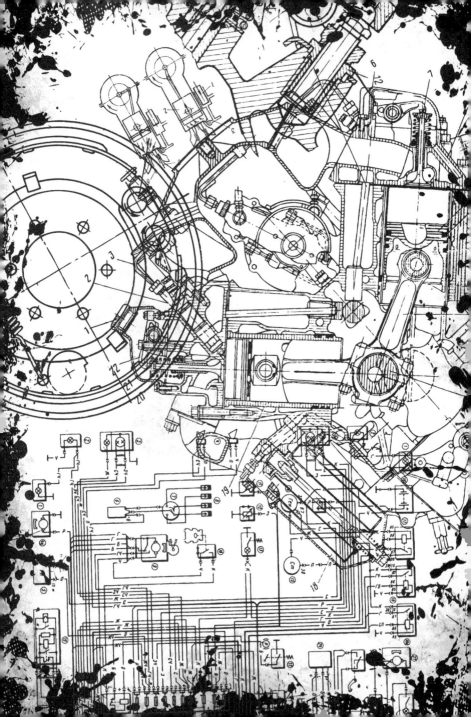

CHAPTER

1

How could Dawk have possibly known that one mouse could break down an entire army? Carthaginian soldiers were supposed to be super tough guys.

The Carthaginian leader, Hannibal, was a super tough guy, so the men in his army should be too. They were bringing elephants across the Alps, after all, and were well on their way to a rampage through the Roman Empire. That wasn't a job for cowards and weaklings. It wasn't a job for scared soldiers.

At least that's what Dawk thought, but the chaos around him said otherwise.

His younger sister, Hype, was behind a boulder with Mom and Dad to avoid the flailing soldiers and trumpeting elephants. The whole scene was pandemonium.

The elephants are out of control. (Dawk)

Watch out for the tusks! (Link friend)

Throw some peanuts! (Link friend)

Nice knowing you. (Link friend)

Real funny. His friends on the Link were not helping. Dawk wished they would stop talking to him for one one-hundredth of a second so he could figure out his best move to safety. Between their comments about his current predicament and babbling on about their adventure in some vReality PlayMod, he couldn't think straight.

Mom snapped him out of his confusion.

"Dawkins Faraday, you get over here this instant!" Dawk's mother, Professor Zheng Faraday, screamed over to him from behind a boulder.

She did not look amused. Neither did his father, Professor Abulcasis Faraday.

Because of Dawk's little prank, Hannibal's entire sweep through Rome might not happen. Dawk knew that this would probably change history, but he didn't know *how* it would change history. They could return home and find out that temporal technology had never been invented and that they were all living in mud huts.

Changing history was a big deal.

"Care to explain what just happened?" Dawk's dad asked.

"And start at the beginning," his mom added.

Dawk sighed. That was a very, very difficult thing to demand of a time traveler.

◎◆◎

As field researchers for the Temporal History Research Division of the Cosmos Institute, Dawk and Hype's parents had devoted their lives to gathering all knowledge ever—literally anything you could know—and compiling it onto the NeuroNet of the twenty-fifth century for all citizens of the world to access.

As you can imagine, they met lots of interesting people. Like Carnelian, a soldier Dawk and Hype befriended over games of Ur in the evenings during the long march through the Pyrenees.

The brother and sister had been taught to play Ur by Carnelian, but had also picked up pointers by searching NeuroPedia and asking friends on the Link. The Link was the social side to the NeuroNet, and the time travelers' neural bypasses in their brains were able to access it even when time traveling. This meant that at any time they could bother their pals for the most obscure knowledge and sometimes advice.

NeuroNet was designed to be a very important tool for the survival of society. One portion of the neural bandwidth offered constant access to any data at any time, and let anyone who wanted to cross-reference it, add to it, whatever they needed to do. It was like tuning into a shadow world in your head that could access a hard drive with the storage capacity the size of a solar system.

It was always there. No one ever found themselves not knowing something. Access was that simple.

NeuroNet was also everyone's favorite form of fun and chatter. It carried official communication, but also personal ones, which was nice since you couldn't leave the Alvarium because of horrible conditions on Earth outside, and also because you hardly ever saw other people during the course of the day in the twenty-fifth century. It kept everyone less lonely. The Link had been created to handle all personal traffic so the entire NeuroNet wasn't overtaken by it.

NeuroNet was also the only way to access vReality modules for learning or for fun. PlayMods were for fun and the more important of the two to most kids.

Maneuvering NeuroNet was as simple as focusing your thoughts, which is why meditation became a key part of the early education process in the twenty-fifth century. Preschoolers learned that they could train their brains to do all sorts of craziness, including compartmentalize. That meant creating sections of the brain that could only be accessed outside the mind by special permission. That is how people kept their embarrassing thoughts from spilling out onto the Link, and so far no one had figured out a way to hack into those.

Yet.

Dawk just let it go, though, a constant chatter shooting at him from the future to wherever he was. It could be a little distracting, but it also got him immediate help with real-life problems when he needed it quick.

Like with Ur, his favorite game.

Winning at Ur was not quite as simple as sending out requests for help, but that didn't hurt. Dawk and Hype's unusual skill at the game had strengthened their friendship with Carnelian. By the time the army had hit the Alps, the siblings had taken to marching with him.

On this day, Carnelian had motioned to the horde of elephants that Hannibal had brought along. "What makes me fearful," he'd said, "is that we have brought these beasts to face against a great force, but it only takes the slightest of creatures to send them in furious retreat."

Dawk and Hype had shrugged at each other. Dawk was half listening to whatever Carnelian said and half tuning into a group in a PlayMod about ruins on a mysterious island inhabited by dinosaurs. His buddies were running through it and he was tossing out directions, playing on the sidelines, and wishing he could dive in. Of course, he could have played along, but marching over the Alps wreaked havoc on his concentration with PlayMods. He usually ended up a spectator to his pals having all the fun.

"Can't say we really know what you're talking about, Carnelian," Dawk said.

Carnelian rolled his eyes. "Obviously that Rome is a filthy city, and with filth comes vermin, and our great elephants are no match for the most unassuming of vermin."

"He's saying that the elephants could be scared away by mice," Hype explained, tossing her hair. "Carnelian, that's a myth. You have nothing to worry about. The elephants don't have to fear Roman mice."

"About that, you are wrong," Carnelian said, shaking his head, "but to prove it, I will make a wager. If you are right, I will carry your waterskins and packs all tomorrow. If I am right, the two of you will somehow manage mine on your backs."

Dawk and Hype eyed each other, searching for some reaction in the other that would give permission to make that bet.

What do you think? (Dawk)

Safe to make the bet? (Dawk)

Hype's Link silence allowed Dawk to be the first to speak up. Maybe she knew there wasn't a point in trying to talk him out of it.

"Sure, we'll take that bet, but how are you going to prove it?" Dawk asked.

This guy is betting a mouse will send an elephant running away in tears. That's not a real thing, right? (Dawk)

If we had elephants or mice anymore I'd tell you. (Link friend)

Carnelian pointed a short ways back to the army physician and his medical cart. "He has what we need."

I can't believe I'm about to do what I'm about to do. (Dawk)

What are you about to do? (Link friend)

What I'm about to do. (Dawk)

Dawk went over to the doctor's wagon. Among other strange items, he spotted a cage of mice.

"Could I?" Dawk asked the army doctor, pointing at the little rodents. "Carnelian has a, um, wart on his back, and it needs immediate attention."

"I'll mash it up for you," the old man grumbled, but Dawk reached for his arm.

"No, no," Dawk said. "My sister will do that. You are too busy attending to warriors to worry about me."

The physician nodded in agreement, reaching into the cage and grabbing a mouse for Dawk, who thanked him and ran back to his sister and the soldier.

"Got it," he said.

"Toss it over there," Carnelian said, motioning to the elephants.

Throwing a mouse in front of an elephant might seem cruel in some future eras, but Dawk figured the poor thing counted as good as dead here anyway, thanks to the physician. It would be the mouse that was scared and scurry off fast to freedom, not the elephant. Dawk was, in reality, freeing the mouse from a horrible fate as a Carthaginian remedy. Suddenly, he saw himself as a freedom fighter for rodents.

Do mice fly? (Dawk)

Yeah, and they nibble your hair. (Link friend)

Playing toss-a-mouse? (Link friend)

It was still with some hesitation that Dawk tossed the mouse at the elephant, and he felt relieved when the elephant didn't do much. It just marched on by as the mouse scurried past, happy to be free and fleeing.

The soldier marching behind the elephant was another story, however.

As the mouse tried to cross the line of humans and elephants that clumped along through the Alps, the little thing found itself about to be kicked by a foot. Its solution was to hop on top of that foot and cling for dear life, hoping to grab a moment at some point when it could leap back to the ground and go find a boulder to hide behind until everything passed.

Unfortunately, the foot that kicked the mouse

belonged to a soldier. The man could face some of the biggest and meanest warriors on the battlefield, but he was intensely afraid of little rodents. Sometimes he had nightmares that mice were chewing on his toes.

This was his worst fear come true.

"He's eating my foot! He's eating my foot!" the soldier screamed.

Killer mouse on the rampage! (Dawk)

Throw some cheese at it! (Link friend)

The noise was disturbing enough to the elephants, but the soldier's panicked movements stirred them into a frenzy. The elephants did not like one bit the spectacle of the usually grim Carthaginian warrior hopping about on one leg while he waved his foot as frantically in the air as he could manage.

The elephants stopped, then backed up, cautious of the madman in front of them. The handlers tried to calm them down, but as other soldiers ran to find out what exactly was eating someone's leg—maybe there was a lion attacking—the elephants went into full panic mode.

Before they knew what had happened, a

confused elephant stampede was descending upon all the marchers.

Are elephants dangerous when they're mad? (Dawk)

Everything's dangerous when it's mad. (Link friend)

Like parents. (Link friend)

And that's the point when Dawk heard his very angry parents screaming for him from behind the boulder and he ran for cover next to them. Dawk was almost as tall as his dad, but he made himself as small as possible.

"Care to explain what just happened?" Dawk's dad asked.

"And start at the beginning," his mom added. "Don't leave anything out."

"Do you mind if I tell you what happened after the elephants calm down?" Dawk asked.

"Actually, the situation is bad enough that I've let the tech guys know," Dad said. "We need to get out of here and go home."

"That is," Mom added, "if our children haven't done something to change history and therefore the future and the tech guys don't exist anymore."

The air took on a strange quality behind the

boulder, like space itself was becoming wrinkled. This was the time doorway that the tech guys had opened up for them. It was like looking through water—you could see what was behind it, but it was a distorted view. Everything rippled and the doorway moved closer to the family as the tech guys on the other end—in the twenty-fifth century— maneuvered it to them.

Dawk was still looking for familiar faces. There was no sign of Carnelian, but he did spot the mouse ducking behind the safety of a small pile of rocks.

That made Dawk feel a little bit better. Then he stood calmly as the temporal shaft moved around him and his family, and they went back home.

CHAPTER

2

When they returned to the twenty-fifth century, the tech guys still existed and history had not been changed. Hannibal and his soldiers had managed to get the elephants under control and continue onto Rome. PlayMods were still the number one thing for anyone to do. No mud huts. Dawk was relieved. They hadn't messed things up too badly.

Hype went on NeuroPedia to see how history remembered the elephants in the Alps. There was one story—unconfirmed—that an elephant rampage had caused a rockslide that led to trouble for the crossing. That was a relief, but Dawk wasn't surprised. As any seasoned temporal researcher knew, it was incredibly hard to actually change history.

But that didn't mean they weren't in trouble. People were laughing about it all over the Link and, therefore, in Dawk's brain. Constantly. He knew more about the incident from monitoring it over the Link than he did from living through it.

The family was met at their return by a tiny, glowing, spherical OpBot that Dawk thought hovered near their heads in a very judgmental way.

"Greetings, Faradays, and welcome back to the future, which thankfully still exists unscathed, no thanks to you," the OpBot said. "We thought for a moment that you might have inadvertently prevented the invention of pie through some strange series of connections, but after tracing it back, we realized that pie still did exist, it was just that the central Nutrofabricator data bank needed a reboot. Once that was done, it was pie for all." The little robot seemed to raise its nose in the air.

OpBots weren't standalone robots. They were

sensors for IntelliBoards. IntelliBoards were artificial intelligence chips, housed deep in the safety banks underneath the Alvarium. OpBots were their eyes and ears in the real world. And apparently, this IntelliBoard had become devoted entirely to poking sly fun at the Faradays.

The OpBot went on. "Of course, it does not help matters that the incident revealed the gloom of a pie-less world, showing the humans in the Ruling Cluster what might be if something did go wrong. It unsettled them. Being artificial intelligence, I could care less about pie, but I know how humans are about their flaky delicacies."

The Faradays could hardly get in a word edgewise as the tiny, floating smart aleck with the very audible vocal chip led them through the pathways of the huge enclosed city, the Alvarium, where they lived.

Since conditions on Earth had gone from bad to even worse, everything was inside the Alvarium. That included the Faradays' employer, the Temporal History Research Division of the Cosmos Institute.

Dawk had never been outside the Alvarium—except, of course, when he was time traveling.

"The Chancellor has demanded to speak with you," the OpBot told them. "I worry that he'll rethink the whole family assignment system, but based on my sensors, I am happy to put in a good word. Dawkins doesn't look half as troublesome as the Chancellor said he was. Then again, my understanding of human nature has been programmed into me. By humans. And that programming tells me that appearing not so bad is a common trait shared by most of humanity."

The OpBot stopped outside a small door. Dawk recognized it as one of the Chancellor's Kiosks, rooms used for face-to-screen meetings with the Chancellor. You had to do something really bad—or really great—for the Chancellor to want to meet with you.

An elephant riot on Hannibal's march was probably not something really great.

"Please be seated," the OpBot said. The Faradays found seats on small benches outside the door. "The Chancellor will call on you via the Link, and only then may you enter the Kiosk. Good day."

And the little bug of a bot flitted off.

The family sat in silence.

I feel bad for Carnelian. (Hype)

Dawk made a face.

Really. We just have to face the Chancellor, but Carnelian is probably standing before Hannibal right now—or then. And Hannibal freaks me a lot more than the Chancellor. (Hype)

Mom and Dad scare me more than any of them. (Dawk)

Mom and Dad weren't very happy, but as the family sat outside waiting for the Chancellor, their faces stayed reasonably brave and sympathetic. They hadn't asked who had brought the mouse on the treacherous march. Now that the family was safely out of the danger of elephant trampling, there was no point in laying out blame.

"One thing's for sure," Dad said, breaking the silence. "They're not going to reassign us to a zoo."

Enter, Faradays. (Chancellor)

The room contained several benches, and one wall was covered with five screens. The words "In Recess" were on each of them. A microchippy version of the national anthem started up and the image on the central screen changed to show a blue chicken wearing a police helmet.

No one knew what the Chancellor—or any member of the tribunal—really looked like. The members were only known by their Avatar symbols and their screen names.

Animated Avatars were passed down in families for centuries, and were often the source of fights and even court cases. Possession of the Avatar signified being head of the family. You could pay to have a family Avatar crafted that you could pass down your own branch. Some people did that, with the hope that it would become important at some point in time. But most people just used free Avatars.

Now that the Link existed, hardly anyone needed an Avatar anyway. What was the point of a digital face when you could communicate with thoughts?

"Faradays, it did not seem reasonable to pursue our inquiry via the NeuroNet," the blue chicken said. "I felt a face-to-screen inquiry was more prudent."

And terrifying. (Hype)

"Abul," the Chancellor went on, "I understand

your family created a dangerous temporal incident. In fact, it was dangerous enough that you left your assignment."

"There were trampling elephants everywhere, sir," said Dad.

"And these elephants kept you from seeing the incident through?" asked the Chancellor. "They kept you from making sure a temporal anomaly did not take place?"

Dad looked flustered. "Well, your honor," he began. "I can only guess that you have not only never seen an actual elephant, but you've never seen a panicked actual elephant pounding through crowds of human beings that seem little more than—"

"I will note that as an answer of 'yes,'" the Chancellor said. "It is also my understanding that your family actually caused the very danger that sent you fleeing from your duty."

"That is less certain," Dad began.

"No," said Dawk. "It's certain. I'll take responsibility for that."

Dawk's family all turned to gawk at his

announcement. Dawk had never done anything like that, ever.

Hype smiled and spoke up too. "But he shouldn't have to, because I was there with him. I should have stopped him, or at least said something to the Carthaginian soldier who encouraged Dawk to toss the mouse."

"Carthaginian soldier, you say?" asked the Chancellor. "Do you have a name for him? I might like to do a personal timeline audit, just to make sure we've been thorough."

"His name was Carnelian," Hype said.

"Thank you," the Chancellor said. The blue chicken Avatar did a little jig and flapped its wings. "This makes my decision a simple one. You will keep your jobs. However, you will be on probation, since this incident did rank fairly high on the Anomaly Scale. Your next assignment will have much less opportunity for disaster. Until further notice, the Faraday family investigative team shall do their duty within the Historical Footwear division, which is currently in need of a specialist in lacing techniques and sole density."

Dawk groaned.

The Chancellor wasn't done. "I am also forced to take the extra precaution of assigning an escort to your children. This is to avoid any potential trouble. And now, in the matter of Temporal Mischance and Recovery Number 400773, that is all. Please try harder."

And with that the screen went blank, leaving a momentary silence in the room.

"Shoes?" whispered Dad. "I don't know anything about shoes."

"You wear them," Hype said, "and that's at least a start."

CHAPTER 3

After lunch—fabricated chicken product with creamed cellulose, which was much better than it sounds—the family climbed onto the sidewalk and rode it back to the Cosmos Institute Kiosk clusters, where they would pick up their new assignment.

While they waited, Dawk and Hype were arguing. That's what Mom and Dad said, anyway, but the two kids swore they were having an intellectual conversation.

"If we did actually change history, we wouldn't get in any trouble because whatever we changed it to would be the new history," Dawk said. "The people in the future beyond that moment would never know events had originally been different. Next time, we should hang around until history does change, and then we won't get in trouble."

"Next time?" asked Mom. "You're planning a next time?"

"It better not involve any elephants," said Dad.

"I'm not sure your logic makes sense, anyway, Dawk," said Hype. "There are plenty of researchers who say you can't change time, and that anytime you try to, what actually happens is you create a parallel universe that diverges from your own at the exact moment you changed time. Which turns into a huge mess. Better come up with a new plan."

Dad looked disgruntled. "If that's true, then I don't see why we just got assigned to the footwear division. According to that theory, it's impossible to do what we just got in trouble for."

They waited outside a Kiosk for a few minutes. The door swung open, and Benton walked out. Benton was the setup guy. He made all time transitions smooth. He would reveal when they were traveling to, why they were headed there, what dangers they needed to be on the lookout for, and how their Visual Cortex Shells would be programmed to show to the temporal natives of the era.

Visual Cortex Shells were the key to time traveler survival, since they helped people from the future blend in with the past. The Shells also made sure that the Cosmos Institute didn't have to keep a collection of costumes for their agents to choose from, which would be a waste of space and resources.

The principle behind Visual Cortex Shells was simple. It was a trick of the light. When a person sees something, anything, what they are seeing is not the thing itself, but the light bouncing off the thing, going into their eye, and being processed by their brain. The shell was a body suit made up of visual cortex alternators. Those tiny little sensors could be programmed to change the light bouncing off of the suits. Then the light was processed by viewers' brains so that they saw whatever the programming dictated. The setup could even be used to make a person invisible. It was all in what you told the visual cortex alternators to make the body suit look like to others.

To fit into whatever era they entered, the Faradays didn't just change their clothes. They changed the color of their hair, and skin, and eyes. In the twenty-fifth century, of course, those things didn't matter. But in the past, they did.

Benton wasn't just a byte pusher, making sure every traveler looked the part. He was also a time traveler, with plenty of time agents under his command, and he had already set in motion the circumstances for the Faradays' arrival. His actions changed things, but not too much. Those actions were known as temporal inconsequentialities, which meant they ranked as very low impact on the history-changing rating system, the Anomaly Scale.

"You'll be landing in the on-again, off-again capital of the Holy Roman Empire, Prague, in 1648," Benton said with a smile. "Emperor Ferdinand III will be in the process of negotiating the Peace of Westphalia with nearly every nation in Europe. This marked the end of the Thirty Years' War. He'd otherwise be spending his time in Vienna, but we wanted to catch him without all the intrigue of a usual court setting. He will have a small entourage and be a calm, thoughtful emperor ready to reveal all about his footwear."

"You hear that, kids? We get to see a real treaty signed!" Mom said. No one could blame her for at least trying to make it sound exciting.

"No, actually," Benton said apologetically. "The treaty isn't being signed in Prague. Ferdinand has an envoy in Westphalia taking care of that. You'll be in his court, where he is focusing on his musical endeavors while the serious business of peacemaking is handled by diplomats hired for the job."

"What has all that got to do with shoes?" Dad asked.

Benton smiled. "Ferdinand will be on the lookout for new trade opportunities, thanks to the end of the war. One of our agents just spent several months in his court convincing him that shoes will be the next great export for the Empire in this new time of peace. The agent also convinced him that a study is needed to figure out what the ruling class desires in their footwear and how to best fulfill those desires on a wider scale for trade purposes. You are the shoe economy researchers he is expecting."

"And convincing the Emperor to take on shoe economy researchers won't change history?" Dad asked.

"The only thing it changes is what he did with some of his time during his stay in the castle in Prague," Benton said. "A small detail that changes no larger path. Not quite like disrupting Hannibal's march to Rome."

Benton motioned for the family to follow him into the Kiosk. There was a control panel and two metallic poles nearby.

"I'll reprogram your Visual Cortex Shells for the appropriate clothes," Benton said as he moved behind the console. "Anyone have any color requests?"

☉❖☉

Soon, Hype was busy admiring her virtual olive dress on a screen that showed what had been programmed into the shell. At her waist, the dress jutted out in a full circumference that made her feel like a cake or something.

"Let me introduce you to Fizzbin," she heard Benton say to her parents.

"Is that your man in the Emperor's Advisory Council?" asked Mom.

"No, that's Yates," Benton said. "For security reasons, he won't reveal himself to you in any time period except in the case of emergency. We try to avoid beheadings of high-level operatives, don't you know. Training is so tough, we hate to have to go to the bother more often than we have to. Fizzbin is your official escort."

"I've never met anyone with a name like Fizzbin before," Dad said. "What part of the Alvarium does he come from?"

"The robotics lab part," said Benton, as a familiar OpBot hovered into view. "Faraday family, meet Fizzbin, your assigned escort for temporal missions— or, rather, his OpBot. Fizzbin is an IntelliBoard in the main core controlling this OpBot."

"Yes, we've met," Dad said. It was the OpBot

who'd ushered them into the Chancellor's Kiosk earlier. Hype noticed that Dad was doing his best to not show his humiliation at the situation.

"Hello, Professor Faraday," said the OpBot. "It's so pleasant to see you again, and, my, those boots programmed into your Visual Cortex Shell add the illusion of inches to your height and plenty more than that to your dashing demeanor."

The OpBot turned toward Mom. "And the other Professor Faraday, your visage is as lovely as the intelligence flowing through my nodes. You will charm the court in Prague, no doubt."

Hype laughed. Her mother was beautiful—on good days, Hype hoped she looked a little like her—but an OpBot wouldn't know beauty from dirt.

Mom sniffed. "I doubt it," she said, "since I'll be spending most of my time staring down at the floor."

Is this going to be the worst trip ever? (Dawk)

Hype grinned and kept her thoughts blocked.

Time travel was more than just stepping into some wormhole tunnel in one year and coming out into another. Any teaching robot in the twenty-fifth century could tell you what a complicated process it was for the huge equipment Benton ran.

The machines had to collapse the actual dimension of time, scan it to find the place inside the dimension that traveler wanted to go, and rebuild the dimension so the traveler ended up exactly there.

It was all about finding the right nanoparticles that controlled the time flow, disrupting that flow around the general space of the traveler, and then starting it up again with the traveler at a different time.

It was complicated, but Hype understood it.

Her problem was that she didn't enjoy it.

She liked going back to the past, but the process always made her a bit dizzy and a lot queasy. That often meant she couldn't eat for the first day in any new time period. This could be either torture or a gift, depending on where they were.

She was happy that the family's assignments

were going to be more low-key and less filled with action and violence. She wouldn't ever tell Dawk that, though. He liked the action and violence.

"Are you ready, love?" Mom asked, putting her arm around Hype. "Plenty of time for the Link later, dear."

Urgh. Whenever Hype had a look of wistful concentration on her face, Mom assumed she was on the Link. Mom had been raised in a society where the Link was accessed through a behind-the-ear hot spot that you could remove. She still didn't completely trust neural bypasses, and she just assumed both of her children were constantly on the Link. She was half right.

"I'm ready. And I'm not on the Link," Hype muttered.

It was never a good idea to time travel in a bad mood, so Hype immediately worked on thinking of something funny. She thought back to the soldier screaming about the mouse, and smiled as the world she was born in became a blur around her, and then a mess.

The inside of her head wasn't able to grab any

clarity. The less the space outside her made sense, the less her brain had anything to make sense of. The confusion spiraled into total disorientation as it seemed she was standing in nothing and everything. Everything at once. Her brain could only handle so many moments piled up at once into something that felt like infinity.

All moments at once. She doubted she would ever get used to time travel.

Bit by bit, Hype could see it. Grand paintings. Tapestries hanging high. Velvet and flecks of gold made the trappings of the room elegant, candles all around gave it what little light it had, and the stone walls reminded her that castles were always very dank.

"Well, Prague seems a bit gloomy," muttered Dad.

CHAPTER 4

It turned out that Prague Castle was not as much of a dump as it had first seemed, but it wasn't in great shape. Less than a year before the Faradays' arrival, it had been ransacked by the Swedish army. They stole all the statues out of the courtyard and had apparently rampaged through the building.

Clutter and debris didn't make things any more interesting to Dawk, who felt ripped off that the family had arrived just after the excitement. Fizzbin's attempts to explain the history of the Thirty Years' War didn't help the mood much. The war had been very complicated and most of its causes seemed outdated to the Faraday family anyhow.

As they got to know their new station, Hype began taking walking tours of Prague to pass the time. Dawk made a habit of slumping down in the most comfortable chair he could find and starting to stream the Link.

The best chair in the castle was obviously the throne, even though it wasn't in the best shape, thanks to the Swedish army. A couple of hefty alchemy books took the place of the front right leg and kept it reasonably level, at least for the Emperor's purposes.

Once, Dawk went to watch his parents at work down in the throne room where the Emperor did a lot of his business. They couldn't get the Emperor to focus on the thing they needed him to focus on—shoes. Ferdinand kept going on and on and on about the last time he had visited Westphalia to check in with his team on the treaty signing, which coincided with a musical composition he was working on and was excited to share.

"You can imagine I was hardly amused when

Trauttmannsdorff suggested that my tune might well be placed in a larger body commemorating this treaty that has yet to be signed. And in front of the Swedes!" Ferdinand said. "I am the Emperor of the Holy Roman Empire, not some court composer! I left immediately. How could I not?"

"And which boots were you wearing when this incident occurred?" Dad asked without missing a beat.

"The brown ones with the cuffs, I think."

"Of course. The best ones for exhibiting dignity against that sort of swipe," said Mom. "And did Trauttmannsdorff have anything on his feet?"

The Emperor ignored her and got wistful. "Sadly, I left those boots in Hofburg. How I miss Vienna! How I miss livable accommodations! How I miss cuffed boots!"

"Prague Castle is quite grand, your majesty," Dad said, "and the perfect flooring for such comfortable, square-toed shoes."

"Though I hate to think what the dust does to the ribbons," added Mom.

"I confess I do worry about the state of the place

and how the rubble might scuff," Ferdinand said. "I'm afraid the Swedes made a mess of the place."

Dawk looked to the Link for something to pass the time.

What do you do in Prague in 1648, anyhow? (Dawk)

Go get beheaded! (Link friend)

Try on some wigs. (Link friend)

Knock over some statues. (Link friend)

His friends in the future were no help at all.

◎◎ ❖ ◎◎

Hype's tours around Prague had made her days pass more easily.

It was a real fairy-tale city, just like the ones she had encountered in PlayMods that pulled from old stories where tiny people called elves made shoes and magic put beautiful girls to sleep in towers. Prague was that kind of place, and she could walk through it forever.

There was some paranoia in the air that the Swedes would return—there were plenty of statues left in the city that were ripe for the plundering—

but Fizzbin assured her that, according to the history banks, they were safe.

She was actually glad to have the OpBot around. In fact, Fizzbin was the difference between Hype being mindlessly confused and understanding just how interesting her surroundings were.

Obviously she had warmed up to the OpBot much more than her brother had. Having the OpBot along so he could provide stories and history about Prague made him seem like more than a distant computer chip programmed to babysit them.

What's that tower? (Hype)

A magnificent but crumbling structure hung on a hill, overlooking all of Prague.

That's a castle, Vysehrad, to be exact. It's fabled to be the site of the original settlement of Prague—believe that if you want, it's harmless. It was home to royalty until around 200 years ago, before various armies began constantly kicking it about. Of course, that's what armies like to do, and it's what they do best. (Fizzbin)

It's still lovely, even if it is a dump. Sad. (Hype)

Don't be sad. In just a few years, Ferdinand is going to restore it and turn it into a training place for his army.

There will be a citadel and towers. It will be quite grand. In another century it will have underground shafts and a huge room at the center called the Gorlice for the armies to gather. Later it will become a place for people to live. In our century, it is a dome-protected quantum research post populated entirely by SciBots dedicated to uncovering the secrets of the multiverse. (Fizzbin)

Hype couldn't stop staring at the beautiful building.

Suddenly, she crashed into someone. Papers went tumbling, satchels dropped, and Hype looked down, embarrassed, at the man she had knocked over. His mustache was graying but pointed out at an angle, and his head was covered with a pitch-black skullcap. He was dressed in a dark cloak that made him look quite mysterious.

"I'm so sorry!" Hype said. She knelt down and began frantically gathering all the man's belongings.

"No need, no need, I'm late as it is," the man snapped and grabbed his satchel away from her. "You don't keep the Emperor waiting, especially for something like this!"

"Are you going to Prague Castle?" Hype asked.

"I live in Prague Castle! Do you need any help? Maybe I can introduce you to the Emperor!"

The man sighed. "I don't need an introduction, as I already know him, but an extra pair of hands would be appreciated. And if you didn't mind helping me set up my presentation to his majesty, that would surely begin to make up for the disaster you've wrought from thin air."

Hype couldn't tell if he was actually angry or was just teasing her. The hardest thing to get used to with time traveling was how humor changed from era to era. But of course she would help him out. She began carefully gathering up his clutter as the OpBot hovered silently behind the cloaking shield it had manifested.

"I'd be pleased to help you," Hype told him. "I was heading back to the castle anyhow. My name is Hypatia Faraday, by the way."

The man grasped the tips of her fingers lightly. "Pleased to make your acquaintance, Miss Faraday. I am Richthausen, Jan Konrádt Richthausen, mintmaster in Brno. But not for long! Today I secure a position! Today I attain the elevation I have sought for years, the result of my very own genius and sweat!"

Richthausen hurried along and Hype followed, doubling her pace as they barreled through the cobblestone streets of Prague, eagerly pushing passersby aside.

"That sounds exciting!" she said. "And how are you going to do all that in one afternoon?"

"The only way I know how, miss," Richthausen said. "I am going to transform useless metal into priceless gold for the Emperor. And you are going to assist me!"

Finally! Something exciting is going to happen! Dawk, meet me in the throne room! You're not going to believe this! (Hype)

⊚⊚ ✦ ⊚⊚

Dawk was already waiting when Hype arrived, just behind Richthausen. He had already heard the details from Fizzbin, who had cross-referenced the weird man in the history banks and found everything he claimed was true.

It's an exciting opportunity to see a successful alchemist at work. (Fizzbin)

Successful? You mean he actually can change any old metal into gold? (Dawk)

No, no alchemist could do that. Successful as in he received ample reward for fooling the Emperor. Which he will. (Fizzbin)

You're taking all the suspense out of this. (Hype)

You'll get no more spoilers from me about today's event. (Fizzbin)

Hype introduced her brother to the alchemist, but Richthausen only peered at Dawk between the scrolls of paper that the older man carried with him. Then he dropped his pile on a table near the throne and motioned for Hype to do the same with the pile she was carrying.

"We have little time to arrange things properly before the Emperor arrives," he said nervously. "Everything must be placed perfectly so that the presentation dazzles, and so that it is successful, as well." He pointed to Dawk. "You, boy, don't just stand there gaping like a dimwit, unless of course you are a dimwit, in which case you will forgive me! If not, your sister could use some assistance removing the clutter from the satchels."

Dawk wasn't so sure he liked this guy, but he moved over to help Hype anyhow. What was the point in punishing her for Mr. Bossy-mouth's behavior?

Inside Richthausen's satchel was a pile of old-fashioned laboratory equipment. He insisted that it had to be put together under his strict guidance or the transmutation would not work. "Everything must be precise!" he muttered. "This is a delicate matter, which relies on all the parts coming together as one!"

Dawk hated being bossed around like that, but he took Hype's lead when she gingerly began laying out the parts onto the table.

"I hope the master will show patience for such bewildered, shriveled minds as ours as we do his dirty work," she said, smiling. She winked at Dawk.

"Forgive me, forgive my nerves," Richthausen said, and began to help the two assemble an odd collection of copper tubing, smaller phials and one larger vessel, a wooden spigot, a small metal tank, and some sort of apparatus meant to heat the contraption, which involved plenty of clumpy charcoal.

"The Emperor will provide the mercury, which will go up here," Richthausen said, pointing, "and siphon through there, where it will come into contact with my secret ingredient. Have you heard of Anima Mundi?"

He pulled out a tiny pouch and whispered, "My precious powder. I will use a grain encased in wax. The Emperor need not know of my stockpiles quite yet."

Dawk didn't know what Anima Mundi was, even though he could tell that Hype did. Her eyes had widened at the words.

He quickly found information about a myth told by the alchemists of old. The chief job of an alchemist had been to discover how to change any metal into gold, and the fabled ingredient for this purpose was called Anima Mundi.

No such substance was ever discovered, which meant a lot of the men wandering around calling themselves alchemists were swindlers. They often used sleight of hand like a magician to get rich people to believe that they could buy a bit of real Anima Mundi.

Dawk and Hype looked at each other. Just what had they gotten themselves mixed up in, exactly?

Anyone know how criminals are punished in the seventeenth century? (Dawk)

Slowly and painfully. (Link friend)

CHAPTER 5

Dawk and Hype finished helping Richthausen build his contraption. Then the Emperor entered with a small group that included their parents. Fizzbin had reassured Mom and Dad that Dawk and Hype were involved in the presentation with his approval.

It is a very interesting learning experience they couldn't obtain in other situations, was how Fizzbin put it.

It better be, was how Dad responded, his career flashing before his eyes.

"So this is the mintmaster of Brno, come to achieve what so many have tried and failed at," Ferdinand said, smiling.

"Your highness," Richthausen said. He bowed, along with Dawk and Hype.

Ferdinand made a wiggly gesture with his hand. "Oh, pish posh, simply pish posh, sir. On with the transmutation, now. I feel like being astonished today!"

Richthausen nodded humbly and gestured to his contraption. "As you can see, the Still for the Water of Life has been prepared with my two apprentices, and we shall set to work. Of course, your majesty, you have brought the mercury."

The Emperor nodded. A man with a very pointy black beard came forth with a crucible, which he handed to Richthausen.

Richthausen took the crucible, which was filled with mercury, and poured it into the top vessel of the alchemical contraption. Then he tossed some coal onto the already-lit flame underneath.

"The quicksilver will heat to a certain point," he explained, "after which it will trickle down into the lower vessel and be filtered by this: my very important additive."

Richthausen pulled out the little piece of wax and held it up between his finger and thumb for all the court to see.

"No doubt you have heard of the fabled Anima Mundi," he said, "but one detail you did not know is that I, Jan Konrádt Richthausen, have procured that item through my research, experimentation, and effort—an item no other man has managed to harness, an item that will create gold where there previously was none!"

Richthausen moved toward the Emperor and positioned his face so that he was staring directly into Ferdinand's eyes.

"It is a scheme that could make a poor man rich," the alchemist said, "but it is better that someone who knows what to do with the rewards of science have knowledge of its secrets."

Dawk made a mental note to ask Richthausen for some speaking lessons. This guy was good—the ultimate scoundrel.

Dawk suddenly felt confident that maybe they

would actually get out of this safely, and far from dungeons and shackles.

Richthausen turned dramatically from the Emperor and immediately began inserting the little bit of wax into a gasket connecting the tubing between the upper and lower crucibles.

He looked at the Emperor and said, "I have risked life and limb, and witnessed many strange creatures and arrangements, in order to procure the barest amount of Anima Mundi for you, your highness. And today, the tree of my efforts shall bear fruit expressly meant for you to pluck from its branches."

Dawk shook his head. This guy was so good. If this whole alchemy thing didn't work out, Richthausen could be the next Shakespeare.

The contraption's contents were starting to come to a boil, and the room was silent with tension. Emperor Ferdinand looked very patient. If there was some worry beneath it all, his face didn't betray it.

That's probably the sort of thing that qualifies him to be Emperor, Dawk thought. *That and the crown.*

Everyone in the court watched as Richthausen switched the levers in the gasket. Following its contact with the Anima Mundi, the mercury siphoned down into the lower container.

After that flow stopped, Richthausen let the concoction settle further over the second charcoal heat, then dribbled a portion into the lower vessel in order to check on its progress.

"There is far too much crimson in its palette," announced Richthausen. "The proper tint should be greenish, such as envy might appear, and it will require a couple drops of silver to adjust."

Richthausen began patting around his own body, searching for something. "I seem to be short today," he said apologetically. "Anyone? Your highness?"

Ferdinand gestured to his mintmaster, who delivered to Richthausen a couple of tarnished silver coins.

Richthausen added them to the mix in the contraption and settled in for more waiting.

"As you can see," he said, "this is not magic, but science, based in logic and method. It is not luck! Rather, it is knowledge, tested and displayed!"

He placed a mold beneath the spigot of the lower vessel for the hot, liquid metal, and turned to his audience.

"For you, your majesty," he said, giving a slight bow toward the Emperor.

A liquid of light brownish color began to slowly pour down into the mold. The Emperor and his mintmaster stepped forward to take a look.

Slowly, the substance began to firm up, and the mintmaster examined it through various lenses. He sniffed, he mumbled, he shook his head, and raised one eyebrow.

"I've never seen such a thing, your highness," he said, almost hushed with awe. "This gold appears to be twenty-four karats."

"At the very least," said Richthausen, smiling. "Mine is not some shoddy recipe."

"You will find yourself rewarded if this is true," said the Emperor.

"My only desire is for your satisfaction, my lord," said the alchemist.

Dawk inched closer.

Can you do an analysis, Fizzbin? Is the mintmaster

so horrible at his job that he can't recognize a total fake? (Dawk)

The OpBot moved quickly and silently, still in stealth mode, which allowed it to be invisible. It set its sensors to studying the metal cooling in the mold. If an OpBot could show surprise, Fizzbin certainly did as he messaged back to Dawk.

It's not a fake. It's the real thing. That wasn't in the history banks. (Fizzbin)

"Fizzbin thinks this is a good learning experience, does he?" came a voice. It was Dad. He had wandered over from the Emperor's area, and he looked concerned.

"Don't worry, Dad, we're perfectly safe," Dawk said.

"I'm sure you are perfectly safe," Dad said. He lowered his voice and added, "But what about the past? Is history safe? I just hope you're showing some caution while you pal around with shady alchemists from Prague."

"He's from Vienna," Hype corrected him.

"And if he were really shady, I don't think Fizzbin would let us near him," Dawk said.

It's a valuable learning experience for them, and part of my function of keeping them out of trouble is keeping them occupied with interesting activities in any time period we visit. (Fizzbin)

"How befriending a criminal who's trying to defraud the Emperor of the Holy Roman Empire is a learning experience, I'm not sure," Dad said, "but we program IntelliBoards like Fizzbin to know this sort of thing, so I won't raise a stink about it. However, if I find one speck of fake gold solution on the Emperor's boots, the whole project could be ruined, so be careful."

☙ ✤ ❧

Later that night, Dawk and Hype's rooms were dark except for the glint of the moon through the windows. They were both awake in their beds, talking to each other on the Link, tossing and turning.

Just try to go to sleep. (Hype)

I can't sleep. I'm starving! How am I supposed to survive on two meals a day? (Dawk)

When in Prague, you should do as the Praguites, or Praguians, or Praguelodytes do. (Hype)

Most of their back and forth involved stressing out about Richthausen's real block of gold. The history banks had nothing in them to indicate that the block was real. The entire incident was presented as just one more swindle by a fake alchemist.

If the gold is real, like Fizzbin says, then we have to figure out how he did that. (Dawk)

It would be a useful bit of knowledge. The technology to create pure gold is centuries and centuries away. Even though it's possible in our own century, the process results in a degraded form. The alchemical sciences are still in their infancy, even in our time. (Fizzbin)

Maybe he used magic. (Hype)

Any technology from an advanced civilization is indistinguishable from magic to a less advanced one. I believe he used technology from our future. (Fizzbin)

So there's a time traveler involved? (Dawk)

It seems so, yes. And a clumsy time traveler, at that. (Fizzbin)

Why clumsy? (Dawk)

Because he left his Anima Mundi in a place where

Richthausen could find it. That's very unprofessional. (Hype)

But how come no one thinks that Richthausen came up with the technology himself? Maybe he's just that smart. (Dawk)

You are suggesting that he make a sudden leap in science at least a thousand years ahead of his own technology. He may be smart, but I doubt he's that smart. (Fizzbin)

One way to get to the bottom of the mystery was to see for themselves the Anima Mundi that Richthausen had hidden away. Then Fizzbin could analyze it. The likeliest way into Richthausen's house was to get invited for tea, if people actually drank tea when and where they currently were.

That gave Dawk an idea.

Why don't we tell Mom and Dad that Fizzbin has come up with a project for us to study what people serve at gatherings in this era? (Dawk)

I know that there are gaps in our social beverage records. You may consider yourselves assigned. (Fizzbin)

And so it was under that deception that the next morning the Professors Faraday were convinced that it was all right for Dawk and Hype to spend time around Richthausen.

"We'd appreciate a report on your findings," said Dad. "And remember to notice his shoes. That might be interesting, what an alchemist wears at home when he's not busy swindling the Emperor."

CHAPTER

6

Later that morning, Hype decided that taking a stroll through Prague with Richthausen was the perfect way to get an invitation. She started by complimenting him on how amazing his transmutation skills were.

"Oh, it was nothing, really," Richthausen said with a grin. "Just a little flexing of my scientific muscle."

"So the Emperor's mintmaster has verified that it's real gold?" asked Hype.

"As expected."

"I hope this will convince my brother," Hype said. She had rehearsed that earlier.

"Your brother just hasn't experienced enough of the world," Richthausen said. "He has no standard by which to judge technology."

"No, I suppose he doesn't," said Hype. "But maybe you're just the one to give him some perspective. Maybe if he saw how complicated your work is, how much is involved, then he would take his first step into understanding the future!"

Richthausen stopped, excited. "I think that is a very good idea, Hypatia. I could have you both for cha. I have a house at Karlovo Namesti, in Na Morani. Number 40. I would be pleased if the two of you would join me."

A quick NeuroPedia peek told Hype that cha was tea.

Hype was startled when Richthausen began swirling a hand above his head. Hype could just make out a glint of a disguised, hovering OpBot, teetering out of the way. The OpBot hovered around the top of Richthausen's head, out of his range of vision, using the Visual Cortex Shield to appear like a very busy gnat. That was just Fizzbin's way of displaying moral support.

"Filthy insects!" Richthausen muttered. "I feel as though they are following me around today. Me, who by the end of the day, mark my words, will carry a title of far more importance than mintmaster of Brno."

"We would be delighted to join you for cha, Herr Richthausen," Hype said, smiling.

◌◎ ❖ ◎◌

Hype collected Dawk from Prague Castle. Then the time travelers made a dash through the streets to Richthausen's house.

He acts like he's going to be royalty or something. I thought he just wanted money for his show. (Hype)

A title is far more lucrative in the long run. It would give him access to the elite circles of the Empire and that would ensure that the favors would keep coming. In the right circumstances, he might never need money again. (Fizzbin)

Richthausen's neighborhood was far more

crowded than the area near Prague Castle. There were people wandering in the streets, stalls with workers and cattle, fish markets, and places to buy coal and wood. It smelled a little bit. Dawk thought it was about as different from 2492 as any time could be.

Richthausen's house was only impressive because of how badly it was falling apart. Dawk was a little worried when his sister used the door knocker to announce their arrival. Best-case scenario was that the door came loose; worst-case scenario was that the house tumbled down as well.

Thankfully, neither happened. Richthausen just carefully opened the creaking and flimsy door, and peered out. "Please, my dear guests, do come in."

It was dark inside. The entrance hall had scuffed floors, peeling walls, and rickety benches.

"I would apologize and say that my home is no Prague Castle," Richthausen said, "but I know that structure has also withered from its previous glory. Come, follow me."

Dawk and Hype followed him into another room. There was tattered seating, as well as a small table. A tray sat on the table, holding a tarnished metal teapot.

It is never a good sign when an alchemist can't keep his metals polished. (Dawk)

Dawk and Hype sat down. The OpBot hovered nearby, disguised and carefully monitoring the conversation.

In a corner of the room, Dawk spotted the entrance to the place Richthausen obviously spent the majority of his time: his laboratory.

"I know my lodgings are not very impressive, but they have an impressive history among alchemists," Richthausen told them as he poured the tea. "Some of the great alchemical researchers have lived here. That makes it perfect for the sort of work I do. The house does have some strange tales attached to it, though. Unavoidable, given the former residents!"

"You mean ghost stories?" Dawk asked.

"Witches, devils," Richthausen said, cheerily sipping some tea, "that sort of thing. Inanimate lumps of clay brought to life."

"That sounds silly," Hype said.

"It is silly," Richthausen agreed, "until the lump

goes around Prague terrorizing the citizens. But I don't care for any of that. I am only interested in gold and my station in life. I leave creating monsters and conjuring demons to the madmen."

"Speaking of which, we'd love to see your laboratory," Hype said.

"Of course!" said Richthausen, beaming. He led them to it.

Dawk peered into the doorway. He could see cluttered tables of glass canisters, and tubing, and apparatus for small fires, and larger contraptions like the one Richthausen had set up in the castle. The tables were stained from spills, and underneath each was a pile of old books.

"You're a very busy man!" Hype said.

Richthausen nodded. "You don't get to my level of mastery by avoiding the grind of the laboratory, you know."

"Do you mind if I take a closer look?" Dawk asked.

"Please do," Richthausen said with a smile.

As Dawk walked in, there was a pounding at the front door.

"I was expecting no one," Richthausen said, and wandered off to answer it.

"Quick," Dawk said. The OpBot darted from its hiding place and began racing around the laboratory, from beaker to container. It was scanning for residue of the Anima Mundi, the powdered solution that Richthausen had used to make the transformation at the castle.

Nothing.

I detect no materials other than the typical useless ones that an alchemist of this time period would have in the lab. Certainly there is nothing that could even hope to turn any useless scrap metal into permanent riches. (Fizzbin)

Footsteps came toward the laboratory, and the OpBot returned to hiding. Dawk turned to face Richthausen, who was approaching them merrily, with a large parchment in his hand.

"That was a messenger from the Emperor," he said, glowing with happiness. "I am to attend a special ceremony at Prague Castle tomorrow! I am to be made a baron!"

CHAPTER 7

Richthausen became a baron, and his full title was one that Dawk totally envied. The Emperor had proclaimed him Baron Chaos. Right at that moment, Dawk wished more than anything that he could have an awesome name like Baron Chaos.

Dawk and Hype didn't hold Richthausen's good luck against him, even if it might have been gotten through some kind of deception. They had traveled through time enough to see that life used to be really tough for people. Honesty was always the best policy, of course. But they couldn't blame anyone for doing some harmlessly dishonest things to make their lives better, especially in a world before microprocessors and toasters and all sorts of great things that would eventually make life a lot easier.

Also, they were totally enjoying the celebration, particularly the bits and bobs at the snack table.

Richthausen drank from a goblet with others in the court. The Emperor had come to have a word with him.

The Emperor's voice rang out through the room. "Thank you for asking, Baron Chaos! My current musical composition is coming along splendidly! It certainly takes the edge off news of intrigue and nonsense coming out of Westphalia! It is almost peaceful here!"

The Emperor leaned over to Richthausen and whispered something. The movement heightened the OpBot's audio sensors.

"The one annoyance and distraction to my composition work is the two shoe people buzzing about with the constant quizzing and the scribing of notes," the Emperor said. "It wears on one with responsibilities such as I, more so than even the peace of the continent. Surely what I use to lace my boots cannot be that integral to trade!"

Richthausen turned. When he saw Dawk and Hype, a grin flashed on his face. "My supreme lord, I do believe you have met my alchemical assistants?" he said. "Most helpful youngsters, on the pathway to becoming masters of alchemy in their own rights!"

The Emperor bowed his head to them. "A female alchemist?" he said. "What a novelty!"

"I'd say it's about time for a girl alchemist in the ranks, your highness," Hype said. "It's so hard to find a practitioner who can actually achieve everything he brags about, so maybe it's up to the women to make the strides required."

Dawk was impressed. Talking to an emperor like that was pretty brave.

"Indeed, indeed," the Emperor replied. "You're the shoe people's daughter, yes? Alchemy is certainly a better pursuit than footwear, and less annoying. I say, yes! Show the boys how it is done! As you progress in your career, should you require a patron, perhaps we might have a sitting to speak in that regard."

The Emperor nodded at Richthausen. "Expert scouting on future talent, Baron Chaos. Compliments. Now back to the fray."

As the Emperor walked away, Richthausen patted Hype on the back. "That was marvelous," he said, smiling. "You have impressed the highest of the high. And now, I would like to extend an invitation to you and your brother. Tomorrow night, the Alchemist Guild will meet at my home. I would like to officially introduce you to them and help secure your place among your future peers."

"Wouldn't that be pretty risky, sponsoring a girl as a future alchemist?" Dawk asked.

Richthausen shook his head. "I plan to go down in history as a groundbreaker! Never before has an alchemist produced gold of such purity through the secret of the Anima Mundi. Even as I take those honors at tomorrow's guild meeting, I would like to follow those glories with something much more bold."

"Then we'll be there," Hype said.

Richthausen bowed his head and moved along to meet more of the important rich people who were going to help pay for his lifestyle from now on.

"Pretty amazing," Dawk said, complimenting his sister. "I'll go get us some food to celebrate!"

∂◎❖◎ᖯ

As Hype congratulated herself, she felt a firm grip on her shoulder. Fearing something awful, she turned around to face the worst thing she could think of—Mom, with a very concerned expression.

"Did I hear that man correctly, Hypatia?" Mom asked. "You're not really planning on becoming an alchemist, are you? Fizzbin told us this would just be a learning experience. We certainly didn't expect it would turn into a career option! You told us that you wanted to go into temporal academia like Dad and me. You said you wanted to study the history of dance with the hope of reintroducing the practice into our century! Please tell me you haven't given up that dream!"

"Oh, Mom, of course I haven't!" Hype said,

rolling her eyes. "But a temporal dance historian needs to be quick with her brain as well as her feet in order to discover things. We're just pretending to be interested in alchemy in order to get involved in Richthausen's exclusive dance society. It's a whole area that has operated under the radar of history!"

"And your brother is helping you with this?" Mom asked.

"He feels very guilty about the mouse thing," Hype said.

⊙◎ ❖ ◎⊙

Dawk walked around the table of food, trying to decide what to pick. He could never be certain that any given morsel wasn't made out of something horrifying, so he demanded that Fizzbin have the OpBot do an analysis of each dish. It was not encouraging, and Dawk reminded himself that time travelers are bound to eat what time travelers are offered.

There was an Alvarium legend about a temporal researcher who had spent a lot of time in prehistorical eras, and had developed a taste for huge bones of charred meat. He returned to the Alvarium and became obsessed with trying to replicate the food he had gotten used to.

Each time, the Nutrofabricator overloaded and there was a small explosion. It was for a simple reason: bones weren't edible to humans and Nutrofabricators weren't designed to make anything inedible to humans. It was like trying to use them to create shoes or hair or chairs. It couldn't be done, and the Nutrofabricator couldn't handle the request.

The researcher was soon forced into early retirement because of his insistence on blowing up Nutrofabricators. One day, he just disappeared. Some say that he commandeered a quantum transitionary device and went back in time. Others claim he just left the Alvarium, hoping to find a modern equivalent of his favorite dish out in the world.

Kids on the Link were always claiming to have seen the researcher creeping through the Alvarium after the corridors had been dimmed. The Bone

Man, they called him. It still gave Dawk the chills, even though he was too old to still believe in the Bone Man.

Dawk couldn't believe that no one had ever made a PlayMod of the Bone Man chasing the player through the Alvarium. He decided to file that idea away for later.

But he kind of understood the Bone Man. The Alvarium sometimes didn't seem quite like real life. Time traveling did. In the Alvarium, you were never breathing fresh air, or eating real food. Out here, you were.

Even if sometimes the food seemed pretty questionable.

Dawk looked down at the table, trying to decide what to eat. While he stared at the food, he tried to figure out where the OpBot might be.

It was obviously in stealth mode. Fizzbin's presence was easy enough to feel when he was close. The electromagnetic waves that the OpBot emitted gave a slight tingle that you could recognize if you knew what to feel for.

But Dawk felt none.

Dawk, what is currently happening in the corner of this banquet room, far from the food, begs your attention. (Fizzbin)

Show me. (Dawk)

Dawk fixed in on the tingle of the OpBot and followed it through the crowd, across the room, and over to a corner. There, Richthausen was speaking animatedly to two unsavory-looking thugs. One of the men wore a huge violet feather in his dull cap. They both looked out of place in their frayed, gray clothing, next to the fancy styles worn by everyone else in the room.

Any idea what's going on? (Dawk)

It seems the two tough fellows want some property back that belonged to their dead master, a man named Busardier. They say the property belongs to them now. A run through the history banks on alchemy reveals that Busardier was one of the masters of alchemy in the seventeenth century. (Fizzbin)

Do you think Richthausen stole the Anima Mundi? (Dawk)

It's a logical guess. (Fizzbin)

Do you think Busardier was the clumsy time traveler

from before? Do you think he left the Anima Mundi out for Richthausen to grab? (Dawk)

That's far less logical. I'll continue to search the history banks for any small bit of information that can help answer that question, but I doubt there is any. (Fizzbin)

But a time traveler could go back and erase the evidence. A time traveler could rig the history books! (Dawk)

That's why our only chance to figure out what's going on is if we look into it now, while you're in 1648. (Fizzbin)

Dawk smiled. He was starting to like Fizzbin.

CHAPTER

8

Life in Prague was getting more complicated by the minute. As far as Richthausen was concerned, Dawk and Hype were coming that evening in order to officially sign on as his apprentices and shine more glory on his already illustrious alchemical career.

Mom and Dad, however, still thought that their kids were going to study secret dance moves. Hype had told them she'd need a dance partner, and they agreed.

"As long as Fizzbin is involved, I can't see what

kind of trouble Dawk could cause, anyhow," Dad had said.

As they headed to Richthausen's house, Hype was keeping her ears open for anything that had the slightest hint of time travel.

Dawk was eager to spot some kind of alien technology lying around.

Fizzbin would have the OpBot working the crowd, focusing its audio sensors on various conversations in hopes of picking up anything that could be fed back temporally through the Link, analyzed, and then sent back for them to find the time-tripping culprit.

Dawk and Hype plowed through the crowds to Richthausen's home. To really make it seem like she was attending a dance—even a secret one held by a semi-famous alchemist—Fizzbin had needed to adjust the filters in Hype's Visual Cortex Shell to reflect something much fancier than her usual court dress.

"I'm glad I don't really have to wear a dress like that," Hype had said. "I don't think I could dance in something that wide."

As they approached Richthausen's front door, Dawk said, "I don't know if I can go through with this. What do I talk to a bunch of chatty alchemists about? I'll never be able to fake it."

I will monitor your interaction and provide you with conversation notes through the Link. Shut off any other NeuroChans and pay attention. (Fizzbin)

Hype tapped on the door and Richthausen opened it. He was decked out in a black waistcoat covered in strange symbols. "Please, please!" he said, motioning them in.

As soon as Hype and Dawk were inside, Richthausen veered off somewhere. Hype and Dawk looked around. The room was packed with all sorts of men with intense looks on their faces, engaged in energetic conversation with each other. The symbols on Richthausen's coat could also be found on articles of clothing being worn by people throughout the room. The strange clothes competed for attention with the men's huge mustaches and beards.

Many of the men were gathered around a table where food had been laid out. Though quite modest in contrast to the spread at Prague Castle, Dawk spied food that looked familiar—loaves of bread, cheese, slices of cake, and nothing remotely mysterious.

A plump man with flaming red hair and a triangular mustache walked up to them. "I baked that cake in my very own Athanor," he boasted. "You must try it. Many of the fellows in this room restrict their Athanor use to metals, but I see a larger purpose. The cake has the usual ingredients— eggs, flour, all that—but, additionally, the Athanor imbued the cake with universal waves. It is a wonderful cake, a cake of enlightenment, of truth. It is a cake of vanilla." He held out his hand. "I am Bogdan Portaco, alchemist and baker. You are quite young to be practicing the trade."

"We're beginners," Dawk said.

"Baron Chaos has taken us under his capable wing," Hype added.

"Capable?" Portaco sneered. "He's never created anything worth having, ask anyone here. A pretender with airs. Baron Chaos, my eye. He will always be Jan Konrádt Richthausen to me!"

"But we saw him create gold for the Emperor!" Hype said. "We witnessed that!"

Portaco shook his head. "Oh, pish posh, yes, he made the gold, but he did not create it. Tell me, young ones, have you heard of a gentleman by the name of Busardier?"

"Is he famous?" Dawk asked.

"In certain circles," Portaco said, nodding. "In alchemical circles. Famous as the genuine article against which all others are naught but pretenders! Rumor has it that Richthausen paid him a visit shortly before he died. And rumor has it that Busardier's business associates are looking for Richthausen. In fact, rumor has it that they showed up at the Emperor's palace when he received his title. They must be very determined."

"Things travel on the alchemical grapevine pretty quickly," Hype said.

"I'm just going to grab a piece of cake," Dawk said, and moved on.

I have analyzed the cake. Along with the usual ingredients, it also contains mercury residue from his Athanor. I suggest you do without cake tonight. My bread and cheese scans, however, reveal a sumptuous feast awaits you. (Fizzbin)

Score one for Fizzbin. Whatever he was up to, he didn't want Dawk dead.

Dawk looked around for Richthausen. The alchemist was over near his laboratory, surrounded by a crowd of men who seemed to be hanging on his every word.

"The Emperor was speechless!" Richthausen told them. "'No one has ever achieved such a magnificent result,' he said to me. 'I demand your secret, I demand it!'"

"I thought you said he was speechless," Dawk interrupted.

Richthausen frowned. "Yes, well, he said all this momentarily after he was speechless. He was speechless, and then . . ."

"Chatty," Dawk suggested.

Richthausen gave his new assistant a glare that could pierce any gold he had created.

"A word, please," he said, grabbing Dawk's arm in order to pull him away into a corner. "What is the meaning of this?"

I know Busardier's men are after you. (Fizzbin)

"I know Busardier's men are after you," Dawk said. Richthausen gasped.

We have to think of the Anima Mundi. (Fizzbin)

"We should really think about the Anima Mundi," Dawk said.

Is it safe? (Fizzbin)

"You're keeping it in a safe place, right?" Dawk asked.

"Of course it's safe!" said Richthausen with a sniff. "What does a child know of such matters?"

"A child who spotted Busardier's men in the shadows, outside your door, waiting to follow you." It was Hype. She had somehow managed to shake off Bogdan Portaco.

"They are out there now?" asked Richthausen, scuttling to a window and peering suspiciously around a tattered curtain. There was movement in the shadows, next to the coal stall that stood across the street.

"It's likely a jealous fishmonger, looking to sabotage the coal merchant's space and take it for his own," Richthausen said. "That sort of thing goes on here so often, I can't even begin to count the number of petty encounters between tradesmen."

"Look at that feather!" squealed Hype. "Would a fishmonger wear such an ugly violet feather the size of his own leg and hide a dagger under his coat?"

Both children watched Richthausen turn immediately pale.

"Busardier's men," he murmured. "They know where I live."

CHAPTER 9

Richthausen began barreling around his home, shooing the other alchemists out one by one.

"You'll have to excuse Baron Chaos," Dawk interjected at one point. "The Emperor requires him right away for, uh . . . for some emergency dental work."

"Dental?" asked one alchemist.

"He needs fillings," Dawk tried to explain.

"Fillings?"

Amalgams. (Fizzbin)

"Amalgams," Dawk corrected himself. "And only

the Baron can concoct metal of such purity that it may go in an emperor's mouth."

"Why would he want metal in his mouth?" the man asked.

Forgive me, Dawk, this appears to have not been a practice until the early 1800s. This gentleman unfortunately finds you to be incoherent, bordering on insane. (Fizzbin)

Dawk patted the man on the back as he hurried him to the door. "The rich and powerful do very strange things," Dawk said, hoping he sounded convincing. "Don't ask any more questions. You won't like the answers."

Hype, meanwhile, was trying to hasten along Bogdan Portaco, who appeared far too concerned about his cake to leave the premises. "I'm afraid the Baron, as he dashes here and dashes there with his newfound importance, will allow my cake to become stale," Portaco explained. "Really, the party will just move to the tavern and the cake will be enjoyed there equally."

"I'll bring the cake," Hype said. "You just go make yourself comfortable with all the others, and

I'll bring the cake over before I go and help the Baron with this sudden call to Prague Castle."

"Are you a clumsy girl, falling about on the streets?" Portaco asked her. "You'd better not be. I don't like to see my cake bruised. All right, I will trust you. But fail me this once and be doomed to my revenge for all time."

"It's a deal," Hype said, and pushed him out the door.

The room was clear—except for the cake—and Richthausen had disappeared.

He's scampered to his workroom. (Fizzbin)

Dawk and Hype both scuttled into the darkness, past the beakers and tubing, and found Richthausen hunched under a table.

"You can hide in here, but I think those guys outside are smart enough to look under this table," Dawk said.

"You don't understand," Richthausen said. "There is a secret passage."

"Under the table?" Dawk asked.

"No," Richthausen said. "But this controls it."

Richthausen had pulled up several tiles

underneath the table. In the hole revealed by the missing tiles sat a wooden crank. He began to move it clockwise, causing a panel of the opposite wall to move aside.

"Once it is open, it will be on a timed catch that will give us thirty seconds to move through the entrance," Richthausen told them. "Then the spring will release it, the doorway will close behind us, and those fools won't know about the passage. I will give you the signal. Now!"

Dawk and Hype sprinted through the doorway, with the OpBot following behind. Richthausen placed the tiles back quickly and ran to the door as well.

It was even darker in the secret hallway, and Dawk and Hype had no idea which way to go. They knew the OpBot's sensors had already found the proper path, but it was best to leave it to Richthausen to lead the way.

They huddled in the darkness until Richthausen opened a very small cabinet on the wall and pulled out a glowing rock.

"A triumph of one former resident, Edward

Kelley," Richthausen said. "He was an inspiration to us all."

He's ignoring the problem. (Hype)

"Why are you running from those men?" Hype asked.

Richthausen shuddered. "I cannot tell you," he said. "But if they catch me, they will kill me. And they will kill my associates—you—as well."

For a moment, everything was silent.

"I think I hear thumping," Hype said.

"And music?" added Dawk.

"Many strange, invigorating things lurk in these walls," Richthausen said. "And I mean in the walls, where we are now. Ghosts, of course, and the detritus of alchemists past. One legend tells of a black doorway—almost a hole—that can suck you into the nether regions ruled by demons, a decrepit kingdom beyond our world."

Dawk rarely got scared by that sort of nonsense. Ghost stories didn't have much hold on a logical mind raised in the Alvarium. He'd encountered plenty of other supernatural tales in the family's time travels, and none of them ever fazed him. But now, in the dark of an old house in Prague, pitch black except for a strange glowing rock, with two thugs out to get them, he could admit he was at least a little bit bothered. And what was with the sound of the piano gently floating in the air?

"I think I hear clomping," Hype said.

"Um, maybe we should move on," suggested Dawk.

Richthausen stumbled into the darkness by the light of the little rock, which only illuminated a few feet in front of him. As near as Dawk could tell, it was an ancient and weathered space, with cobwebs everywhere and the occasional bump on the foot that led him to think there could be mice or rats crawling around.

What is that? (Dawk)

Rats. (Fizzbin)

The noise from inside the house was getting louder, which meant the thugs were getting closer and angrier. Richthausen moved cautiously, though. The thud of danger could not get his feet shuffling in the dark any faster.

"The staircase is ahead," Richthausen cautioned.

"It is snug. One of us tumbles and we all go down, and then my new title will be useless."

They cautiously began creeping down, and in between the creaks of the steps all of them heard the piano music getting louder. It wasn't music that Dawk or Hype were familiar with, though. It murmured. It was like a murmuring, dizzy piano, with deep tinkles, each one extended and warbling and running into each other.

"Do you hear that now, Baron?" Hype said. "That music?"

"Oh, just the wind blowing through this old house," the alchemist said. "Nothing to worry about."

"I'm not worried. Are you?" Hype asked.

Richthausen said nothing, but by the dim light of his glowing stone, it looked like he was breaking a sweat.

"I feel something!" Dawk whispered.

"I hope it's not slimy," Hype said.

"No," Dawk said. "Something made of wood. It's different from the wall. It's larger."

It's a door. (Fizzbin)

"I think it's a door," Dawk said. "I'm pretty sure. No, it's definitely a door. That's a door if I ever felt one."

Would you like me to scan behind it? (Fizzbin)

"Is this the exit?" Hype asked.

"No, that's further, slightly," Richthausen said. "This must be the Room of Ubiquity."

"You've never seen it before?" asked Hype.

"I've never used this secret passage before," Richthausen said. "I've never needed to flee before."

"I find that hard to believe," Hype muttered.

It might interest you to know that I do register a life-form beyond this door. A large one. Shall we run? (Fizzbin)

"I think we should try to get in," Dawk said.

"Now is not the time to dawdle and diddle," Richthausen snapped. "We are fleeing for our lives!"

"You are fleeing for your life," Hype said. "We're just tagging along. Now hold that little rock closer."

Dawk began tapping the door. "There must be a latch. Or a button. Or a voice command."

If you prefer, I will open this door. (Fizzbin)

Yes! (Dawk)

"I'll just keep at it," Dawk told Richthausen. "Maybe I'll knock something loose."

The OpBot began moving along the edges of the door. Fizzbin directed it to insert opposing magnetic forces in the space between the door and its frame. The OpBot hovered around the bottom of the door until it came to one end, and then upped the magnetic charge. This caused the door to begin rattling, which led to cracking sounds, and then a loud *WHOMP* that caused Richthausen, Hype, and Dawk to all screech with surprise and cover their faces.

"I got it!" said Dawk.

Thanks. (Dawk)

You're welcome. (Fizzbin)

"Let's get in there and find out what that weird music is," Hype said, practically leaping over Dawk to get in the room.

"Wait, there's a—" Dawk's warning was interrupted when a heavy thud on the chest knocked him back and he heard frantic scurrying.

"Did you see that rat?" asked Hype. "The way he went sailing right out of there?"

"A rat? A little rat?" Dawk asked.

You said it was a large life-form! (Dawk)

A rat is big to me. (Fizzbin)

"I think it's gone now," Hype said.

They went into the room, brushing aside cobwebs. They walked toward a small wooden box that sat on a stand against a crumbling rock wall.

Dawk picked up the box. Inside was some sort of music box mechanism, with strange strips of metal crossing each other and eerie vibrations coming out of them.

Richthausen followed them in and immediately ran to the contraption. "I have heard about it, but never imagined it still existed," he said. "Hidden away in these walls! I've wasted too much time. I should have searched earlier."

He fell to his knees, hugging and kissing the instrument. "Mladota of Solopysky, I have found your gift, and now I shall use it to be the most powerful man in the world!"

CHAPTER 10

Richthausen was practically slobbering over the weird box with its odd little keys making the bizarre sounds, going on and on about someone named Mladota of Solopysky, and generally making no sense whatsoever.

"Weren't we just running for our lives?" asked Hype.

"Baron, should we keep going?" Dawk asked.

Richthausen took a deep breath and exhaled slowly. He held his arms out. He closed his eyes and took slow breaths. "It seems the most important discovery of my life has collided with a vile threat to it," he said. "Forgive me, losing myself like that."

"What is this thing?" Hype asked.

"It's the creation of the former owner of this house, Mladota of Solopysky. He was a supreme alchemist who specialized in such hypnotic automata."

Loosely translated, he's referring to robots that can put people in trances. I've no record of such a thing, however, and am prepared to qualify that as gibberish. (Fizzbin)

"What does that have to do with alchemy?" Hype asked.

"Who said it had anything to do with alchemy?" Richthausen said. "Mladota of Solopysky's talents were many."

Over the constant noise made by the instrument, Dawk noticed something. Just above the strange instrument, there was some sort of doorway ripping through space, creating a tunnel that made waves in the air. The three humans in the room cowered from its surprise appearance. Fizzbin worked furiously to figure out what was going on.

I'm getting very strange energy readings. They seem to indicate a temporal event, but they aren't consistent with any we have on record. I need to analyze further. (Fizzbin)

Dawk wasn't sure there was time for that. He felt like he was being forced down by whatever energy the tunnel was spitting out. He suddenly had a terrible headache and felt sick to his stomach. He could tell by looking at her that Hype was going through the same thing.

And then Richthausen went crazy.

"They have come for me!" he screamed, and began crawling to the room's exit.

"You're safe from them. They're outside!" said Hype.

Richthausen turned back to them slowly, an expression of terror etched on his face. "The demons of the house!" Richthausen yelled. "They are guarding Mladota's creation and are coming to get me! I have heard tales of people pulled into demon pits and I will not have that happen to me!"

Richthausen struggled closer to the doorway and began pulling himself out. Dawk and Hype were on the floor behind him, edging to the door and away from the furious weight of whatever peculiar event they had encountered.

When they finally got out of the room, Richthausen was on his feet, starting to run in the dark to get to the exit as fast as possible.

Hype pulled herself up and went after Richthausen, catching up to him quickly and grabbing his arm.

"Let go of me!" he yelled. "Given the choice of demons or thugs, I'll pick thugs every time! At least with them I have a chance to come out alive!"

"What in the world was that?" Dawk asked as he caught up with them.

"Not in this world," Richthausen said. "Not in this world at all. I had feared this about Mladota's contraption. The legends are true and the answers will come later. We can imagine Mladota's final fate. For now, we have this."

Something strange is going on. I'm getting dual signals on the OpBot, and double traces of both of you. I feel as though my NeuroNet access is being tampered with. (Fizzbin)

What would cause that? (Hype)

These ghost signals are interfering. I'm getting two different visual feeds from the OpBot. One appears to be a temporal displacement of the previous signal that has the three of you—(Fizzbin)

Now is not the time. Tell us about it after we move on from the weird demon box and escape the big, mean guys. (Dawk)

Richthausen gestured to a panel on the wall. A little box mounted next to it contained a small crank that he began to turn.

The panel opened slowly to reveal the night sky, and Dawk and Hype hopped through it. Richthausen followed them. The panel zipped shut and once again looked like the side of a building, and nothing like a doorway at all.

"Into the night," Richthausen whispered.

"Where are we going?" asked Hype.

"To Vysehrad," the alchemist said, "where we will find the remaining Anima Mundi and ensure our safety."

The three scrambled down the street, sticking to the sides where the shadows cast a darker net over the night. Behind them, they heard the slam of a door and some scuffling on the cobblestones.

"That way!" came a voice. One of Busardier's men. Dawk groaned. They must have been spotted from the window.

Richthausen still had the little glowing stone and held it up to remind Dawk and Hype. "Follow me. Quickly."

⚬⚬ ❖ ⚬⚬

Soon they reached the outskirts of Vysehrad, near the top of the hill and a crumbling structure. They were well ahead of the ruffians, but they could hear rustling in the bramble below.

"They're getting closer," Hype muttered, and Dawk nodded.

Finally reaching the top, the three crept carefully along a stone wall that blocked any entrance to the grounds.

"Part of the wall has crumbled. That is where we will enter," said Richthausen. "Once we're in, we find the enclosure wall of the watchtower. It's crumbling, like everything in there, so we must show care."

No map is currently accessible. I've double-checked with mission logs and suspect we've never sent any cartographers to that century, only historians. I have some data gathered in the eighteenth century, which appears to show extra structures inside, as well as caves. (Fizzbin)

"What are you talking about?" Dawk said out loud.

"Shhh!" both Richthausen and Hype said.

Also, I'm still looking for the source of the ghost signals and hope I can restore my functionality. (Fizzbin)

"Here," Hype whispered.

She had found the opening, and began to make her way in. The other two followed her. The watchtower was a little further along the winding wall.

"Once we get there, you need to grab the Anima Mundi. Then we dash the other way," Hype whispered. "We need to go clear across and lose those guys."

"We can make our way to Brick Gate and then

down," Richthausen said. "Past the Basilica and the graveyard."

They trudged through the courtyard for a few minutes until Richthausen stopped.

He put his hand on the bricks of the watchtower and moved it along carefully, feeling for a loose piece.

There is something wrong. I am registering the leftover energy of a temporal event. (Fizzbin)

What do you want us to do about it? (Dawk)

Is there anything we could do about it? (Hype)

Possibly not. It may just be an Institute hot spot, but a scan through the banks doesn't indicate any registered site, which does make me curious why these readings exist. (Fizzbin)

Richthausen nervously pried a brick from out of the tower and stuck his hand in the revealed space, pulling out a small sack, partially filled.

He shook it at Dawk and Hype. "This is it," he said. "Now we run!"

"I don't think we're done here," Dawk said. He spotted the OpBot floating purposefully around the tower, using its own visual cortex mechanism to look like a moth. "I've got to watch that moth. It's a very rare species."

"We have no time for this!" said Richthausen. "They surely must be gaining on us!"

Tell him that no thugs can stifle the pursuit of lepidoptery. (Fizzbin)

I'm not saying that. I don't even know what it means. (Dawk)

Please, then, work your way around the perimeter of the tower going counterclockwise. The OpBot is waiting for you at the source of the readings. (Fizzbin)

"Hype, which way is counterclockwise?" Dawk whispered. He'd never learned to tell time on a non-digital clock.

Hype sighed and began to walk around the tower, with Dawk following, until she came upon the OpBot. She peered in closer and began to poke at the brick it hovered around.

"It means the study of moths," she said.

"What does?" Dawk asked as he began to help her with the tapping.

"What do you think?" Hype asked, rolling her eyes.

A brick moved, and together they were able to pry it out.

Dawk reached his hand into the hole and began to feel around. It was a small compartment and he tried to be careful.

There it was. A boxy thing. Human-made material. Definitely not from the seventeenth century.

Dawk pulled it out, and the OpBot shone a light on it.

The item was a small white box that fit in the palm of Dawk's hand. The box had a small touchpad and a confusing red readout that was visible through the smoky casing.

"What in the world is that?" asked Hype.

"I would like to ask the same, and also why that moth has a beam of light coming from it," Richthausen said.

OpBot sensor has your pursuers nearby. Fleeing is suggested. (Fizzbin)

"We've got to get moving," Hype told the alchemist.

Dawk and Hype grabbed Richthausen by the

arms and began shuttling him along the grounds. The three ran, the thugs' fast clomping moving quickly behind them.

Hype took the lead. She steered Dawk and Richthausen away from the fancy-looking church and its graveyard and into a more open area, where there were three huge stones that they could duck behind.

But Richthausen stopped and shook his head. "We cannot hide here," he said. "This is cursed! The Devil's Column is cursed! We must find the Brick Gate! That will take us back down the hill."

Richthausen dashed off into the night, with Dawk and Hype trying their best to stay right behind him.

I have a fix on you and can guide you to possible escape. If you were only there running for your life in another century or so, I would direct you to head for the underground chambers. Unfortunately, those chambers have yet to be built and I'm going to have to make do with— (Fizzbin)

Then save the advice for if we're ever here a hundred years from now! (Dawk)

Richthausen ran toward the gate and pounded on the doors, but they wouldn't open.

"There's no way out," Hype said. "We're going to have to try to talk our way out of this."

"Let me do all the talking," Richthausen said.

"I don't think so," said Dawk.

Busardier's two men came running up, daggers in their hands. They looked at their prey with a mix of exhaustion and annoyance.

"You shouldn't run in the dark with those big blades," Hype said. "If you fall, you could put your eye out, or worse."

"Richthausen, where is it?" snarled the one with the violet feather. "We want it back. You give it back and there won't be too much damage."

"Not too much," said the bald one with the eye patch.

"I don't have it," Richthausen said. "It appears someone got here before me and—"

"He's lying," Dawk said. He turned to Richthausen. "Give it to them. It doesn't matter."

"It matters to me," Richthausen muttered. "I know there is something unusual about you two, and I know that you know far more about alchemical matters than you let on. You and that moth, for instance. What are you after? Where are you from?"

They want the Anima Mundi, right? (Dawk)

"I don't know if he should just hand it over," Hype said.

The history banks lead me to believe that the Anima Mundi is unimportant to this situation. Other than a small grain that Richthausen has pocketed for later use, but not told you about, this Anima Mundi never appears again in the history banks. What does matter is that these criminals will hurt you if you don't hand it over. (Fizzbin)

He pocketed a grain without telling us? (Hype)

That is consistent with the history banks. Please pay attention to the danger at hand. (Fizzbin)

"What is that thing there?" asked the bald one, pointing at the gadget in Dawk's hand.

"That's just a, um, toy. You know, for children," Hype said.

The violet-feathered thug grabbed the gadget. "Complicated for a child's toy," he said.

The bald one reached over and touched the

gadget. "It feels different from metal," he said. His finger caressed the casing until it hit the touchpad portion. The gadget made a bleep and a green light blinked on.

The bald man gasped. "Witchcraft!" He moved his finger around the touchpad slowly. The light went from green to yellow.

"The pretty light changes for me!" the bald man said.

"Oh, no," said Dawk.

And that was all. A burst of energy built up around them and they were gone.

CHAPTER

11

All of a sudden, it was daytime.

The burst of light caused everyone to shield their eyes, and Busardier's thugs dropped the contraption. Thinking fast, Dawk grabbed it from the ground and turned around to escape.

The Brick Gate had changed. Now, matching additions were built on each side of it, each with a doorway.

Dawk grabbed Hype's hand and she grabbed Richthausen's, and they ran into one door and down a dark, winding staircase.

"What has happened?" Richthausen asked, but no one answered.

They ran through a stone-lined tunnel that, soon enough, linked to other stone-lined tunnels. They paid no attention to where they were going. They just went.

Both Hype and Dawk tried to consult Fizzbin on their next move, but neither registered anything from him or even each other. It was as if the temporal connection was out. Or the Link. Or the entire NeuroNet. That was completely unheard of.

Fear slid through both of them for the first time that day, but they continued on without a word.

All that was left to do was to run down a long, dark tunnel and take an occasional turn in the hopes that the bad guys had lost their trail.

"Do we even know what we're doing at this point?" Hype asked.

"We are running," Richthausen said.

They turned into a tunnel on their right and stopped to catch their breath.

"But do we have a plan?" Hype asked.

"Well, we've obviously gone through a quantum

transition, but it was more like a jump than a process, which is weird," Dawk said.

"Your words are gibberish to me," Richthausen said. "It is day, when before it was night. Does this strange event have anything to do with that buffoon handling this contraption you found? And why are you acting so surprised about it?"

"It's hard to explain, honestly," Hype said. She tried to choose her words carefully. "There's no such thing as mobile time jumps where we are from. They haven't been invented yet, though time travel will be a lot easier when they are. In our era, we need all kinds of big machines and a temporal feed from a fixed place to do it."

"So this gizmo has to be from our future," Dawk said.

"What are you talking about? Your era? What do you mean by time jumps? A temporal feed? What's a gizmo?" Richthausen asked.

"Let's run now and talk some more later," Dawk said. "Hurry!"

Hype and Richthausen moved along quickly behind him.

Something was nagging in Hype's brain, though. She kept thinking about a word.

Gorlice.

What an odd word. Where had she heard it before? And why was she thinking it now?

Gorlice. Gorlice. Gorlice.

And then she thought: *Shafts. Gorlice. Underground shafts. Gorlice.*

She stopped and grabbed her brother to stop him too. "I know where we are," she said. "Fizzbin told me about this the first time I saw Vysehrad. We're around a hundred years later than we started. The army is probably here."

"Probably?" Dawk repeated. He pointed, and Hype turned to see a parade of soldiers marching across a corridor. The army was at the far end of the tunnel they were currently standing in. They had almost run straight into them.

"Now which way?" Hype asked.

"Maybe if we could get the soldiers to arrest us, we'd be safe from Busardier's men," Dawk suggested.

"Unless they execute us on sight," Richthausen

said. "We are trespassing in a military area under the rule of the Emperor. Soldiers will not treat us kindly, serve us snacks, and shine our boots, even if I am a baron."

"There's a place called the Gorlice," Hype said. "A huge room that Fizzbin told me about. Maybe if we make it there . . ."

Hype led the dash away from the marching soldiers. She figured if all the tunnels led to the Gorlice, then the Gorlice was most likely at the center of the tunnels. That meant it was the farthest away from outdoor access, and so she'd have to use what sense of direction she could manage in the tunnels to figure out where the center was. Every once in a while they heard boots clomping from one direction or another. It sounded like the thugs were stopping and starting, trying to hear the three running away, but maybe getting confused sometimes by the footsteps of the soldiers. The men weren't any safer from the soldiers than Dawk, Hype, and Richthausen were.

They rounded a corner, and Hype happily pointed ahead to a faint light.

"Up there," she said. "That's got to be it."

"And what do we do once we get there?" Richthausen asked. "Will you miraculously know the way out from that room?"

"Maybe there are charts of the tunnels there," she said. "I don't know. If you have any better ideas, speak up."

Richthausen shut his mouth, and together they jogged to the light. They found a room the size of a small stadium. It was empty except for military decorations on the walls, some flags, and a few stools. It looked like a meeting place.

"Just because I do not know how to escape does not mean that escape is not a good plan," Richthausen said with a sniff. "But then I don't even know what these 'jumps' are, unless you care to elaborate."

"We aren't where we were," Dawk said.

"That is absurd!" Richthausen cried. "We are in the Vysehrad, in a secret underground chamber that the Emperor obviously had created for reasons of security. This is not a mystery."

"These tunnels didn't exist in 1647," Hype

explained, shooting a worried look at Dawk. "We've traveled not through space, but ahead through time, to a year when these catacombs exist. We're in your future. Probably about a hundred years in your future."

"My future?" Richthausen repeated, throwing up his hands. "What do you mean, my future? Why not your future?"

"This is our past," Hype explained.

Richthausen didn't have time to respond. Busardier's men were storming through a tunnel on the opposite side of the huge chamber. Richthausen began to run. Dawk and Hype followed, but they couldn't get far. On the other side of the room, soldiers started marching in, then stopped.

Their commander stared at the intruders. "Who are you?" he demanded. "What are you doing here?"

"We aren't with them," the man with the huge violet feather in his hat snarled. "We're in pursuit of them! They stole our property! Our master left it to us and they took it."

"This is your reason for trespassing in a royal military site?" the commander asked.

"We have a right to retrieve what's ours," the bald thug said, scowling. "Even if we have to follow them into the Emperor's dressing room and beyond!"

"And what of you three?" asked the commander, turning toward Dawk, Hype, and Richthausen. "What do you have to say to these charges?"

Dawk tried to examine the situation quickly. There was only one way out. He pulled the time travel gadget out of his pocket, making sure neither the soldiers nor the thugs noticed. Then he turned to his sister and the alchemist. "Baron, Hype, I feel so light-headed. You might want to grab me before I pass out and crack my head open on this hard floor."

Hype frowned, but Dawk widened his eyes at her, and they both did what he asked, taking hold of his upper arms. As soon as he felt their hands on him, Dawk swiped the touchpad. A burst of energy built up around them and they were gone.

CHAPTER 12

"You three! Excuse me! What are you doing there? Reenactors are to meet at the Devil's Pillar to receive their assignments!" The woman was dressed in a crisp blue uniform, very neat, with her hair pulled back into a severe bun. The soldiers and thugs were gone, and instead the room was full of statues.

"We're in the Gorlice, ma'am?" asked Hype.

"Yes," the woman said, hands on her hips, "and that is one place you shouldn't be. Tour groups will be coming through soon. Unless you are assigned to play your historical role in this location, and I doubt that you are, you will follow me to the correct meeting place."

The woman stomped off, her heels clicking on the floor. The threesome followed and attempted to keep up.

There were lights in the room, so it was easier to see. That should have made it a lot less creepy, but the statues were weird. They all looked ancient and stern, as if they knew exactly what Dawk and Hype were up to.

". . . originally placed on the Charles Bridge, but moved here for safety . . ." came the voice of a man dressed exactly like the woman. He was being followed around by a group of people of various ages, mostly wearing shorts. Dawk, Hype, and Richthausen hurried past them.

The huffy woman continued on through the tunnels as if she knew where she was going. The tunnels were damp and cold, but much less menacing than they had been the last time the trio ran through.

There was still no Link access. The clutter that

was usually barreling through Dawk's brain was missing. It wasn't quiet in there, though, since he had a lot of thinking to do about the latest problem.

"I honestly don't know where they find you lot," the woman said with a sniff. "I'm not sure this reenacting hubbub is a good idea. 'History comes alive.' What nonsense. History doesn't come alive! It is represented through lazy loafers and simpletons who don't even know where they're supposed to be and when they're supposed to be there. History is enough alive in these walls without bother like yourselves."

Dawk didn't know what she was talking about, but he knew it wasn't a compliment.

"I'm not quite sure what we're supposed to do next," Hype whispered to Dawk. "I'm estimating late twentieth, early twenty-first century, which means whatever you touched on the gadget, it was wrong. But we want to go the opposite way."

"Why do you estimate the twenty-first century?" Dawk asked.

"The fashions. The shoes. The hairstyles." Hype sighed and shook her head. "I do retain some things I access on NeuroPedia and in the vReality modules."

"At least we left the bad guys back in . . . whenever that was," Dawk said.

"Late 1700s, probably," said Hype.

Richthausen was not taking this so casually. He looked like he was going to have a panic attack. There were plenty of things contributing to this reaction, but mostly it was all the people walking around with metal things pressed against their eyes or black boxes pressed against their ears, as well as the flimsy wires stuck in them. It was all early technology to Dawk and Hype, but unthinkable to Richthausen. Nothing in his alchemical studies could have prepared him for laptop computers. Or short skirts, for that matter.

But Dawk was enjoying the break. No Fizzbin. No soldiers. No marauding goons with fancy feathers. Unfortunately, he knew it was only temporary.

"The sooner you can utilize that tiny magic block to transport us back to our proper state of being, the better, I say," Richthausen said.

"That's worked well for us so far," said Hype.

"It's as easy as transforming useless metal into gold."

Richthausen glared at her.

The woman suddenly stopped walking. "Join them, please, and your supervisor will round you all into action at the appropriate time."

She was pointing to a small group of people crowded around some huge, odd stones. The people were dressed—more or less—in the same style that Dawk and Hype's Visual Cortex Shells already reflected from their positions in 1648. They all looked very bored.

The large stones made the scene doubly strange. Obviously this was a marker of some area of importance—three rods jutting out of the ground, creating an impression of a circle. It struck Dawk that he had seen it before. Something about it was very familiar.

They joined the crowd, not quite sure what they should be doing.

"You seventeenth century? Or maybe sixteenth?" a young guy asked Richthausen.

"You are speaking to me?" Richthausen asked.

"I'm around then," the guy went on. "It was awesome! Golden age of alchemy under Rudolf II! Edward Kelley and all that! So awesome."

"That era was not all it was cracked up to be," Richthausen grumbled. "The years following, however, yielded leaps and strides in the field."

"Oh, no," the guy said, "that time was awesome. That's why I auditioned for the reenactor job. I research alchemy. I thought immersing myself in a role might push me to take it to another level."

"You are interested in taking your alchemical lessons to another level of inquiry?" Richthausen asked, suddenly perking up. Dawk figured he was looking for an assistant who'd be less disastrous than the Faradays.

"Well, I take it as a metaphor for change," the guy explained. "Not really turning metal into gold, but like a parable for all sorts of other transformations that happen, you know like in art, and—"

Richthausen stopped him. "What if I told you it is no fable? Creating gold is about creating gold, nothing more."

Hype grabbed Richthausen and pulled him

aside. "What do you think you're doing, Baron?" she whispered.

"This young gentleman is interested in the craft!" he replied, trying to pull away. "And since my two current aides seem to have other diversions that I had no knowledge of when I took them under my wing, I was merely—"

"I know you don't completely understand this," Hype said, "but we're time traveling. That's a very complicated and delicate thing, Baron, and the less you say to people in this time period, the easier time we're going to have keeping it from getting more complicated and delicate than it already is."

Richthausen kept quiet from then on, though he didn't have much to do but gawk at all the odd things people carried around and wore.

Dawk and Hype, meanwhile, were huddling over their own odd thing, the gizmo that had sent them careening through time in a haphazard way. "What are those little circular places?" Hype asked.

Along the bottom of the gadget, three little glowing green circles had appeared through the casing. Little triangles slowly moved around each circle, like they were measuring something. The numbers, meanwhile, were adjusting themselves backward. Dawk kept moving along in one direction, watching the triangles and numbers change.

"That formation there," Dawk said, pointing at the rocks. "That's the one we were crawling under in the dark, trying to escape from your two friends. From the readings on this thing, I wonder if this is a polarity reverser beacon. Creates a slingshot effect in time travel. Everything's moving backward on it."

"I don't really understand those words, so I must ask simply if it will return us to our proper time," said Richthausen.

"It's not precise, but that's the general idea," Hype said. "I say we test it."

She clutched Richthausen's arm. The alchemist winced, eyes shut, and held his breath.

The atmosphere got wavy around the three, and Vysehrad and the people in it very foggy, until everything turned into total shreds and was finally gone. A wobbly feeling swept through the travelers. This time, it lasted longer than any of the previous jumps they had made.

Dawk closed his eyes.

"Well, this all looks very 1648 to me," came Hype's voice. "I think we're back in your Prague, Baron."

Dawk opened his eyes and saw that they were.

CHAPTER

13

Once they had made their way down the hill and back into the city, Richthausen was noticeably calmer, and soon, animated. It took a while, but Dawk and Hype managed to make him understand that Busardier's men had been left in another time about 100 years from the moment they stood there, and that he was now safe. Time traveling could be very confusing if you weren't used to it.

"You are telling me that the Anima Mundi is safe from those two? That it is all mine?" Richthausen asked.

"We're telling you that we're all safe," Dawk said.

"This is wonderful news!" said the alchemist. "I want to be able to use the Anima Mundi freely! Now that I am a baron, I can't live in that ramshackle house! I can't wear these tattered clothes! My shoes are an embarrassment! The Anima Mundi will fund all that, and more."

Dawk and Hype decided to stick with Richthausen for a while. The Link was still down, so they had no access to Fizzbin. The alchemist's only current idea was to return to his laboratory and whatever nefarious plans he had. Dawk decided that they could figure out how to get the Anima Mundi from Richthausen's possession after a nap.

They walked toward Richthausen's house. But suddenly, Richthausen gasped and stopped. "Have you lied to me, my little friends?" he muttered. His face paled.

"I don't know what you're talking about," Dawk said. Then he saw what had spooked Richthausen so much.

There was a man waving to him, walking

happily over, flanked by two other men. As they came closer, Dawk could see the violet feather in one of the hats, and then an eye patch on the balding fellow. He didn't recognize the third man.

Hype and Dawk stared at each other. How had Busardier's thugs gotten back to their own time?

"Ah, Richthausen!" boomed the boisterous, gray-bearded fellow. "So glad to see you, my friend! I did not know you were in town or I would have insisted you come over for a session!"

"I have only just arrived, Bu-Bu-Busardier," Richthausen stuttered.

Busardier!

Alive!

If Busardier was still alive, they were in the wrong time. They'd missed their proper temporal spot by days—or even weeks. They had not met the thugs yet. They had not been chased through time yet. Busardier had not died yet.

"And who accompanies you today? Servants? Students? Your children?" asked Busardier, staring at Dawk and Hype.

"My apprentices," said Richthausen, smiling

nervously. "Keen to learn the craft, lucky to learn it from me."

Busardier laughed. "Please, accompany us to my home, dear Richthausen," he said. "I would like to welcome you from Brno with a refreshment. We have so much to talk about. Prague is alive with the energies of the cosmos and I procured a goat for a little extispicy. I know you'd like to see what's in your future!"

"Nothing would give us more pleasure," Richthausen said, grimacing.

"Extispicy?" Dawk whispered to Hype. "What's extispicy?"

His sister shrugged. "Whatever it is, I think it's going to end up being more trouble."

⊙◎ ❖ ◎⊙

Busardier might have been a practicing alchemist, but he was also a successful merchant. That meant his home was far more livable than Richthausen's, and the array of food laid out in his living room was much more elegant. After the chase, both Dawk and

Hype were famished, so they were glad to see the piles and trays of food available to them.

As Dawk and Hype shooed Busardier's new goat away from the food, Busardier and Richthausen talked all sorts of alchemical nonsense with each other. That just made Dawk's mind wander. The last piece of the mission was getting the Anima Mundi from Richthausen.

A full stomach helped Dawk think more clearly about that.

The history banks lead me to believe that the Anima Mundi is unimportant to this situation, Fizzbin had told them. *This Anima Mundi never appears again in the history banks.*

Which meant that as far as the historical records of NeuroPedia and the history banks within the Cosmos Institute knew, this Anima Mundi stayed hidden forever.

That was interesting.

"Well, Richthausen, shall we take the goat and peer into the coming age?" Busardier asked.

"That is why I came," Richthausen answered. He looked nervous, like a man waiting for a judgment.

"I must get the instruments." Busardier grinned and left the room.

"What's going on, Richthausen?" Dawk asked.

"You see, Busardier is a fine gentleman," Richthausen said, sighing. "Those two fellows don't reflect their master at all. Of course, they were doing what they wanted when they came after us. I don't have high hopes for what Busardier will do once he sees the future and sees me with his Anima Mundi, however."

"About that," Dawk said. "I have an idea. You're going to need to hide the Anima Mundi until you know you're safe from them."

"I thought I was safe," Richthausen said, narrowing his eyes. "You two said they were trapped a hundred years from now because of your little magic box."

"You never know if they'll find a little magic box in that time, do you?" asked Hype.

Richthausen shook his head. "I suppose not."

"The safest place is right under their noses," said Dawk, "in Busardier's house. It's safe here. We know from our own experience that no one finds it here but you, right? You have it now, and you found it in Busardier's house, right?"

"Yes," Richthausen said, frowning.

"Well, let's look at this logically," Dawk said. "Since we have traveled to a time before you found the Anima Mundi, if you hide it here now, it will also be found later by you. You hid it for yourself to find. Your past and your future are the same."

"I don't understand," Richthausen said.

"Let me try," Hype butted in. "Several weeks from now, you are going to take the Anima Mundi from this house, correct?"

Richthausen nodded.

"That Anima Mundi is the same Anima Mundi that you carry with you now, right?" Hype asked.

"Yes," Richthausen said.

"Well," Hype said, "how do you think it got there—will get there—for you to find?"

Richthausen looked tentative. "I . . . put it there . . . here . . . now. And then in a couple weeks, I will go back . . . and retrieve it."

"Exactly!" Hype said, clapping.

Richthausen didn't really get it; that much

was clear. But he went along with it. He found a dusty little corner behind a chair, pulled the wood molding back, and stuck the substance in for safety with the knowledge that he would be back to get it soon, and that would secure his title and future, and the two thugs would never know.

"Now is the time, my friend!" Busardier said, bursting back into the room. "Let's find out what is yet to come!" He was grinning madly and clutching an ornate and threatening gold dagger.

❧

Busardier led Richthausen back to his study for some mysterious ceremony, leaving Dawk and Hype with all the snacks—as well as their own panic.

"No one can really predict the future, right?" asked Dawk.

"No," said Hype. "I guess it's possible to see the future, you know, travel to it, witness it, come back, and tell everyone about it. That seems a little like predicting it. But I don't think there's any other way to accomplish it."

"So we're safe?"

"I think so."

There was crashing in the back room, followed by Busardier yelling. "Get the creature, you great buffoons! Hold it, hold it! It is but a tiny goat, its horns can only break your skin slightly!"

With a very concerned look on her face, Hype got up out of her chair. She began rummaging through the books on Busardier's shelves. She grabbed one and showed it to Dawk.

The Methods of Extispicy, 5th Edition.

Hype opened it up and began rapidly tearing through the pages. "Oh, no, I had a feeling," she said. "We've got to stop this!"

"What?" Dawk asked.

"They're going to use the goat's entrails to tell the future!"

"That's impossible," Dawk said. "You can't see a goat's entrails! Those are on the inside! How are they possibly going to see—"

Then his face paled. "Oh," he whispered.

They both went racing to the back room and opened the door. The goat came bursting out and dashed madly around the sitting room, kicking over food and candles and furniture.

Busardier's two men tried to move quickly, but tripped over each other and tumbled to the ground. The goat, panicking, ran toward an open window and went flying out of it. Both Dawk and Hype ran up to the window, expecting the worst, only to see the goat safely making its way through the crowds and down the street.

"You will get my property back immediately, Richthausen!" Busardier growled. "If you do not return with my goat, you will get a visit. And when you do . . . you will know trouble."

CHAPTER
14

After a very brief goodbye, and a promise that they would get Busardier's goat back, the threesome made their way back to the streets of Prague. They didn't know what to do with themselves, or where to go; they were too busy trying to straighten everything out in their heads.

"So, they were after the goat all along?" asked Hype.

"Apparently, yes," Richthausen said. "Of course I believed that it was the Anima Mundi when they first approached me, but I could not figure how they knew about it. Busardier's night nurse had summoned me to his deathbed. The two thugs weren't around. They were probably out somewhere, probably up to no good. The attending nurse found my name and residence on a piece of paper lying next to him, and came to fetch me. Busardier must have been going over his accounts when he fell ill."

"Then how did you know where to find the Anima Mundi?" asked Hype.

"I heard rumors that he possessed such a treasure," Richthausen said. "Alchemy is ruled by symbols and codes. It is not hard to use those tools to track down another alchemist's materials, even in his own home. And about the Anima Mundi, I still don't understand how I am supposed to—"

"We've got some other things to deal with, Baron," Dawk said. "We'll straighten out temporal logic for you once all the important things are worked out."

There was still the little problem of having landed again in the wrong time and what to do about that. They had arrived earlier than they wanted to, but not so early that it was worth risking another jump. They were so close. It could all go wrong again.

Dawk and Hype chattered frantically to each other as they hurried through the streets of Prague. Richthausen just walked alongside, struggling to keep up with them.

"Remember when we were in the room with the automata?" Dawk asked. "That weird music box thing? We need to get as near there as possible. I remember Fizzbin saying that he'd recorded some sort of temporal event there, but didn't have time to fully analyze. That's got to be significant somehow, doesn't it?"

"You think that's our key to get home?" Hype was intrigued. "We could always just wait around here with Richthausen for a few weeks, show up at Prague Castle a little after the moment that we leave. Mom and Dad would never know the difference."

"I thought of that," Dawk said. "But do you really want to hang around with Richthausen for a few weeks?"

"You've got a point there," Hype said. "The music box is our best bet."

The three made their way through crowds and stalls before finally reaching Richthausen's house. Richthausen was overjoyed and began to amble up the steps, but Dawk and Hype both stopped him.

"You can't go in yet, Baron," Hype said. "You don't live there yet."

"Yes, I know that," he replied, sniffing. Dawk smiled. It was pretty obvious that the alchemist didn't know that at all.

Dawk pulled out the little gadget they'd found. "It's picking up something. Look," he said. He pointed to its screen. Numbers were continually adjusting as he moved it closer to or farther from the house. The green circles had reappeared, but this time, the triangles inside them were moving in the opposite direction.

Neither Dawk nor Hype was totally sure what it all meant, but it seemed that when different numbers changed, something was going on. Just to see what would happen, Dawk began swiping his thumb slowly along the touchpad portion at the bottom. The numbers slowed down. Some seemed brighter than others.

"My guess is it's latching on to high-energy points in the temporal wave around the house," Hype said. "Right? You're Mr. Temporal these days."

"That's probably it," Dawk said. "We won't know until we activate."

"Do you think we should?"

"It's that or stick around here for a few weeks," Dawk said. "What could possibly go wrong?"

Hype looked out at the shacks lining the street. She imagined having to beg for meals from them. Nothing about that seemed remotely appetizing.

"Okay, get it going," she said.

"One minute," Richthausen said. "I do have a right to know what you are planning. I still understand a few things about a few things, and before you place my life in jeopardy once more, I demand you hand that doodad over to me, as the adult in the party, and—"

"Sorry," said Dawk, "but you're not getting the doodad."

A green light blinked on as the red numbers

swelled from the casing, and then a yellow light. Then the waviness returned, along with a blinding light that only faded as Dawk, Hype, and Richthausen found themselves engulfed by a dark tunnel filled with fuzzy particles that pinged around them with such speed that it blurred their vision of each other, making all three flicker like static as they were pulled forward in the black passage.

At the end of the tunnel, they saw something very clearly. They saw themselves. The three of them—past versions of them, that is—were on the ground. They looked a bit afraid. They were crawling away from the opening, frantic.

"Wait until we disappear," Hype said. "Then move quick."

She grabbed Richthausen and Dawk's hands and waited. As soon as the figures at the end of the tunnel had moved out of view, she quickly moved forward.

It was like being dizzy and falling, except with the feeling that someone was controlling the spiral so they would not be dumped unceremoniously and dangerously on the ground.

And then they were there, with the reality of that moment melting into their visual perception, and the tunnel disappearing in a small ring, then nothing.

Hype put a finger to her mouth and stayed on the ground, very still.

"What in the world was that?" came a voice outside the room, alongside rapid footsteps. They disappeared into the dark distance.

"It's safe now," she said.

"I just saw myself fleeing from demons," Richthausen muttered. "How can that be?"

Something strange is going on. I'm getting dual signals on the OpBot, and double traces of both of you. I feel as though my NeuroNet access is being tampered with. (Fizzbin)

Dawk and Hype didn't know how to respond to that.

Of course, they hadn't known how to respond to it an hour or so ago, the first time Fizzbin said it. That was when they were on the run from Busardier's men, which was happening right about now to their past selves.

These ghost signals are interfering. I'm getting two different visual feeds from the OpBot. One appears to be a temporal displacement of the previous signal that has the three of you— (Fizzbin)

And then silence.

"I'm not quite sure what to do about Fizzbin," Dawk said.

"We should just let him know we're back," Hype said.

"I think he does know," Dawk said. "He's picking up two different OpBot feeds and we've registered twice each on the Link for him."

"That's because our past selves are here as well as our current selves," Hype explained.

"I know. How do we hide that from him?" Dawk asked.

Hype shrugged. "I don't think we need to."

She spotted the automata music box sitting on the pedestal, just as it had been the last time she was in the room. She grabbed it before Richthausen could remember. Whatever the thing really was, it was better to give it to twenty-fifth-century scientists than to let Richthausen fool around with it.

"If we just tell him what happened, he'll handle it," she said.

Hype was right.

Fizzbin took it all in with the logic she expected. He resolved the situation by saying he would act normally when communicating with the earlier Dawk.

The current Dawk offered to give the earlier Dawk some advice, but Fizzbin pointed out that he didn't need any—somehow, despite all the confusion, what had happened had happened. Dawk didn't need to hurry it along.

It appears the automata works as a temporal beacon for time travelers. I can't say who the beacon was built to help, but the device you found must have fixed on it and it responded with a more precise temporal landing site. If you actually knew how to work it, you probably could have engineered it better. (Fizzbin)

How could someone in the seventeenth century have made a temporal beacon? (Dawk)

Maybe someone from the seventeenth century didn't. (Hype)

"Right about now, our past selves have probably

run out of the house and onto Vysehrad," Dawk said. "The two thugs are right behind them and on their way to being trapped a hundred years in the future. Hopefully, nothing will mess up what's already happened and our past selves will loop into our current selves like they're supposed to. Anyhow, the coast is probably clear."

So Dawk, Hype, and Richthausen found themselves going back through the dark and out the exit to the same place they had about an hour before. They were tired from the adventure as they headed down the street toward Prague Castle.

Suddenly, Hype extended her arm and stopped the others. There were footsteps behind them. They were being followed.

"You there! I've got you now!" came a barking voice. All three, sure it was Busardier's men somehow finally there, turned around, ready for trouble.

It was Bogdan Portaco, and he looked very angry.

"I knew you would forget to bring the cake," he snapped.

◦◎ ❖ ◎◦

It was late when Dawk and Hype arrived back at Prague Castle. The Professors Faraday were waiting for them in their chambers.

"Why have we just gotten a message from Benton that we are being called back?" Dad asked.

He looked neither angry nor relieved. Mostly curious. His expression didn't change much after Dawk and Hype explained what had happened, with interjections from Fizzbin.

There was silence after the explanation. Even the Link was quiet.

"So there were no temporal dance studies after all," said Mom.

"I'm not quite sure how to react to this," Dad said, "especially considering that it's all happening just as we were getting the hang of this seventeenth-century shoe thing. Is the Chancellor aware of all this?"

The Chancellor knows what has happened and congratulates Dawk and Hype on their action and discretion in the matter. The temporal items in question have been gathered and will be delivered to the Chancellor following your return. The larger investigation of who might have placed them in this time period will shift to the number-one slot of the Chancellor's priorities. (Fizzbin)

"And will the Faraday family perhaps play a larger part of this priority?" Mom asked. "Not that I don't enjoy footwear."

My understanding is that the Chancellor has no plans to shift assignments currently, though this might be a point in your favor that could speed the disciplinary action along. (Fizzbin)

"Who are all of you speaking to?" asked Richthausen, who they had forgotten was there. "Are you hearing the voice of this Fizzbin person the children keep mentioning?"

"Not quite hearing," Hype said. "More like feeling. His words are just in your head and perceived. That's how the Link works."

"Most miraculous, this Link," Richthausen said. "Like so many other wonders you have explained to me."

"Baron, we're going to ask you to stand back now," Dad said. "You're going to see us fade away. Tomorrow the Emperor will awake to find we have gone to give our report to the trade minister. I'm sure he will be happy to have us out of his hair. We certainly appreciate your silence about what you've learned."

Richthausen nodded. "But of course."

Dawk and Hype both shook hands with Richthausen, who turned out to have much more guts than they initially thought he would.

And, Hype thought, he really had taken all the time travel in stride, though he did look longingly at the automata as Dawk held it.

෬◎ ❖ ◎෬

Richthausen watched as the Faraday family faded away in a slow flickering movement. They seemed frozen, as if statues were disappearing in front of him.

They were gone.

Richthausen quietly took to the corridors and

began to exit Prague Castle. He would now go to Busardier's to retrieve the Anima Mundi, and get moving on some other plans. He had all sorts of ideas in mind.

CHAPTER 15

Nearly a month later, Baron Chaos sat silently in the coach as it ran over the rough roads leading to Solopysky. It was not far from Prague Castle, and he had much to gain from the journey.

He had realized almost immediately how the children had outsmarted him. The bulk of the Anima Mundi was now out of his reach. The boy had tricked him into placing it into a time loop that he could not enter. He understood that much.

The most magical thing about the Anima Mundi was that it had no beginning, no end. It came from nowhere and went nowhere. It was trapped in time, in Richthausen's pockets and Busardier's walls, only able to serve its intended purpose once, and then be doomed to a temporal prison forever.

At first, Richthausen thought that he needed to uncover the secrets of time in order to get the Anima Mundi back.

But then he realized that if he uncovered those secrets, he would have more power than any Anima Mundi could give him.

He had retained one grain, and used that for a further demonstration in the court of the Emperor. This had provided him with more resources.

And now he was on his way to Solopysky to set his plan into action.

He could hear people wandering the streets outside the coach, but did not let them break his concentration. He had plans, and he rolled them over in his mind through the brief trip.

Soon, the coach stopped and the driver climbed down to open his door.

Richthausen stepped out onto the muddy ground and walked up to the door of a house. He knocked twice, softly, and when no one came, once more, with force.

An older woman answered the door.

"I seek Mladota the Younger," he said, smiling at her.

The woman brought him to a modest but comfortable waiting room. "The master will see you momentarily," she said.

Richthausen waited. He investigated the various toys he found around the room, homemade bits of automata made to amuse children. Then he sank into a comfortable chair.

Finally, an elderly gentleman came into the room. He had the general air of a scholar.

Richthausen rose to greet the man.

"You asked for the younger," the man said. "When put up against my father, I am the younger."

"And you continue his work?" Richthausen asked.

"Quietly, for my own interest," Mladota said. "I have no interest in fame or even financial assistance, which makes me wonder what your visit would ever have to offer me."

"I am Baron Chaos," Richthausen said, smiling, "an associate of Busardier in Prague and a member of the court of Emperor Ferdinand III. Perhaps you have heard of me?"

"News does reach us here eventually, Baron, yes," Mladota said. "To what do I owe this courtesy?"

"As an alchemist, I have had some recent good fortune," Richthausen said, "which led me to my current position and much acclaim. I wish to use all my influence and means for something that will move the world forward."

"And how do I come into this?"

"I would like to collaborate with you in your work," Richthausen explained, "and help you take it far beyond any point you imagined."

"And why would you want to do this? Glory? Intellectual interest?"

"I do it because I have encountered your father's work firsthand," Richthausen said. "I know from my own experience that the ideas behind some of his more precise creations are sound. Your father's efforts were, and will be, of great value in the future." Richthausen smiled and breathed deeply.

"Work with me, sir, and we will go far together. The future awaits us."

CHAPTER 16

The Alvarium was the same. Really, it never changed. Ever. It was white and gray and spotless and safe and dependable and a little bit boring. As usual, the Link was filled with chatter about how PlayMods had progressed in the time Dawk had been gone—a few days his time, just to keep his inner clock at balance with the movement of his present.

Forgive the spoiler, but the history banks have no further record of Richthausen following his second performance before the Emperor. Whatever happened to him is of little consequence to the past, present, or future. (Fizzbin)

Did you know that all along? (Dawk)

Of course. I have to monitor these things, to see if your involvement is affecting reality in any way. (Fizzbin)

But how would you actually know if history had been changed? (Dawk)

Temporal backups sent to a manufactured pocket universe designed to hold the data outside of time that can be accessed at any moment to check for changes in time. In other words, I have it covered. (Fizzbin)

Temporal backups? Dawk had no idea such a thing existed, but he decided to take it as proof that he had done the right thing. Creating a time loop in order to perpetually trap the Anima Mundi was the best he could do under the circumstances.

Dawk did feel bad about tricking Richthausen. The poor guy was going to return to Busardier's and realize that he had already stolen the Anima Mundi that he placed there. He couldn't steal it twice. Time was annoying like that.

At first, Dawk worried that his little time loop was going to get him or his parents in trouble again.

Creating time loops could be considered a serious offense, especially since it might be evidence of time-traveler tampering.

There was no trouble, though. The Chancellor could send someone to take a sampling of the Anima Mundi without upsetting the loop that had been established. The technology of the Anima Mundi, as well as the time-jump gadget, was years ahead of what they were capable of. So it must have come from the future. Hopefully they could figure out who had interfered with the past.

"You will be visiting Ancient Rome next," the Chancellor told them. "We're very keen on sandals."

Boring assignment, but interesting backdrop. Dawk and Hype weren't disappointed. And maybe it would even be sunny.

Dawkie, Dawkie, Dawkie! Polluto-zombie time! (Link friend)

Dawk couldn't wait to get to Rome and be under the sky again.

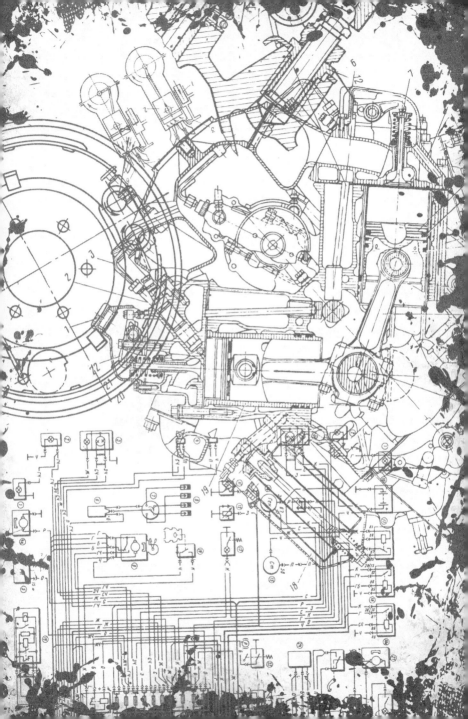

ABOUT THE AUTHOR

John Seven grew up in the 1970s, when science fiction movies and TV shows were cheap and fun. His favorites shows were *The Starlost, Land of the Lost,* and *Return to the Planet of the Apes,* and he loved time travel most of all. John collaborated with his wife, illustrator Jana Christy, on the comic book *Very Vicky* and a number of children's books, including *A Year With Friends, A Rule Is To Break: A Child's Guide To Anarchy, Happy Punks 1-2-3,* and the multi-award-winning *The Ocean Story.* John was born in Savannah, Georgia, and currently lives in North Adams, Massachusetts, with his wife and their twin sons, Harry and Hugo, where they all watch a lot of *Doctor Who* and *Lost* together.